THE GR]
O]

Daniel Scott Buck

Daniel S. Buck

iUniverse, Inc.
New York Lincoln Shanghai

THE GREATEST SHOW ON EARTH

Copyright © 2004 by Daniel Scott Buck

All rights reserved. No part of this book may be used or reproduced by any means, graphic, electronic, or mechanical, including photocopying, recording, taping or by any information storage retrieval system without the written permission of the publisher except in the case of brief quotations embodied in critical articles and reviews.

iUniverse books may be ordered through booksellers or by contacting:

iUniverse
2021 Pine Lake Road, Suite 100
Lincoln, NE 68512
www.iuniverse.com
1-800-Authors (1-800-288-4677)

This is a work of fiction. Names, characters, and incidents are a product of the author's imagination.

ISBN: 0-595-33427-X (pbk)
ISBN: 0-595-66921-2 (cloth)

Printed in the United States of America

THE GREATEST SHOW ON EARTH

For
Kristian Williams

A philosophical joke:

Eat shit. Ten billion flies can't be wrong.

Contents

Chapter 1	THE DRAMA QUEEN	1
Chapter 2	CAROL PORTER SERVICES (CPS)	9
Chapter 3	THE DYSFUNCTIONAL FAMILY	21
Chapter 4	THEORY OF EVERYTHING	32
Chapter 5	THE CONTRACT	45
Chapter 6	SWINE	55
Chapter 7	911	63
Chapter 8	THE WOMEN'S SUPPORT GROUP	73
Chapter 9	ANOTHER DAY, ANOTHER ALTER	83
Chapter 10	DENIAL	92
Chapter 11	THROW IT AGAINST THE WALL AND SEE WHAT STICKS	100
Chapter 12	THE MANSION OF SALVATION	109
Chapter 13	BILL HOWARD'S REALITY TV LAW & ORDER	118
Epilogue	STOP AND SMELL THE FLOWERS	131

Chapter 1

THE DRAMA QUEEN

A black fly knocks against the window glass and drops to the windowsill. Other flies crazy-eight throughout the apartment. A spider knits a web on the ceiling without my permission. The hammer and roar of traffic pollutes my space. Then there is Meme, standing in front of the life-size mirror checking her profile. A white fur coat brings out the pale tone of her face and the mirror reflects the city behind her. From where I'm sitting, it looks like there is an opened door to another Meme and another city. This thought really fucks with me: one Meme is one too many for me. I don't know if that's true. But to watch that fly take a dive, that's nice. It's a beginning, a first step in the right direction.

"There really is nothing out there, nothing that matters," Meme says, admiring her reflection in the mirror.

The phone rings. Meme looks my way.

"I'll get it," I say.

"Don't," she says.

The answering machine speaks her father's voice. It reminds her of the family reunion and asks her to call when she gets in. I walk to the window and light a cigarette.

"How long is this going to go on?" I ask.

Meme primps her red hair and tucks it behind her ear.

"Frank, don't start!"

"All I'm saying is that you are going to talk to them sometime, so you should get it over with so you won't have to worry about it."

She ignores me and continues to admire her face. A song by Billie Holiday comes on. I take a drag off the cigarette and put my face up close to the window and exhale and watch the smoke billow and ripple across the glass. I sit down in a chair and look around my little studio apartment, at the cluttered mess from the half-opened boxes Meme moved in yesterday—marking her territory. My studio practically looks like her old bedroom in her parents' house. A poster of Marilyn Monroe hangs above my red ripped velvet couch. A glamorous Madonna strikes a pose in a poster next to Janis Joplin, who is wasted, slamming a fifth of whiskey.

The beginning of a tantrum appears on Meme's face. She sounds out each breath to get my attention. I swear she thinks her cryptic fits are a phenomenon not to be missed, like comets or shooting stars.

I lift my hand to my head and place a thumb and an index finger on each temple. I strain my head back and stare at the ceiling. I try to block everything out, to pretend this isn't happening.

Meme isn't really going to move in.

A year ago, we had big plans. We met one night at the Polis Club through a guy named Geber. We were buying, he was selling. He introduced us. Meme was by far the most beautiful girl to pose in the dark crowded den of gothics, ravers, and punk girls with shards of silver stabbed in the folds of their faces.

In our ecstasy-induced bliss we prophesied a future as ultra-celebrities in film and poetry. Meme was to acquire some Greta Garbo status in Hollywood and I would be world-renowned as some reclusive gothic poet unveiling the complex fortress of my mind and heart. We were supposed to be famous and living on the French Riviera by now. This diva would cast a spell on the masses and I would secretly compose odes and sonnets in praise of her majesty.

Maybe I should blame the ecstasy.

It kept our dreams alive night after night. Strung out mornings stretched the vision of our life-long dreams, distorting it into a vacant stare on our faces. All the hype would amount to our unspoken embarrassment that seemed to be saying, "Who are we kidding?" Our silence would end with a quest for drugs and the vicious circle would begin afresh, our wishful thinking more grandiose than before, our sobriety more punishing and severe, sticking with us like an unshakable bad mood.

Last week I unsuccessfully ended our relationship. I turned her to face me, looked into her eyes and said for the hundredth time: "This is over!"

She pulled a razor from her drug pouch and scratched several red lines on her wrist. They were really no deeper than a scrape from a rose thorn.

"I'll kill myself," Meme said, "and you'll be a murderer."

Meme moans, failing to raise my eyes in her direction. She adds a whimper.

Still no attention.

She sniffles.

Nothing.

I'm entranced by a fly banging its head on the window, trying to get out. I hear the bed creak from what I'm guessing is a body slam against the mattress. I turn my head and see Meme staring down at the fur wrapped around her neck.

"What's wrong?" I ask.

Meme lifts her head up, her pale face now has some color, blushed pink around her cheeks. We stare at each other.

"What am I going to do?"

"I don't know."

She wouldn't like any of my suggestions anyhow. I've been through this too many times to care. It's like endlessly watching the same bad movie.

"I don't want to wash dishes or make hamburgers!"

"There are other jobs."

"I shouldn't have to put up with this shit."

"You did take his money," I say. "You did take his credit cards."

"Oh, please."

She lights a cigarette.

"Every day it's another traumatic episode in the life of Meme," I say. "I can't deal with it." I comb my fingers quickly through my dark brown hair, noticing in the mirror that my face is as pale as Meme's and my eyes as dark and hollow. "There are other people. Lives other than your own. You are not the center of the…"

"Shut up."

She blows the cigarette smoke in my direction.

I look out the window. It's a hundred degrees out there. The only sign of people outside—the sound of cars passing.

"All I'm saying," I try to think of what I'm saying, "is…maybe…maybe things could be a little more," searching for the right word, "quiet."

Meme shifts to the other side of the bed so she won't have to look at me. Her dark red hair is tangled in the white fur on the back of her coat.

"So what are you really saying?" she asks, not turning around to look at me. "Are you saying you want to break up again?"

Like that would change things.

"Meme," I say, "what am I supposed to do? We broke up, remember? Then you move out of your parents' house and into my place because you got busted. They are not supporting you anymore and you are not doing anything but being a serious bitch to me! I'm sorry that you didn't get the part, I really am, but it's not the end of the world and you are acting like it is."

Meme pushes herself off the bed. She's sweating and red in the face, opening and closing her mouth. This is the kind of silence I've been talking about.

Meme struts across the hardwood floor, doing everything she can to keep from saying something back. She slams the bathroom door behind her. I hear objects crash and bang in there, caught in the whirlwind of Meme's emotional tornado.

Meme auditioned for a part in a big film production, only to be dismissed less than ten seconds into a three minute scene. Opportunity had knocked in the form of an audition notice. Looking back on it now, Meme probably would have been better off without the up front and personal realization that life is not fair: some women got it, some don't; one woman's gain is another woman's loss. In ten words: Meme is not everything she cracked herself up to be. But it was something to live for. It gave her some focus. It gave her herself to talk about with some glitter around the edges. All that reckless energy now cast in the direction of me and Meme's family was nicely honed in on a harmless delusion.

We celebrated the entire night before the audition, anticipating Meme's arrival into the spotlight of spotlights.

"When this film is wrapped up I think I'll move to New York and star in a Broadway production," Meme said. She casually puffed a cigarette. "Maybe I'll just move out to Hollywood. It's really a hard decision to make, you know. Broadway or Hollywood?"

Things were hopeful. Meme confidently petted the collar of her mink coat and talked about picking a record company, Warner Bros. or some other label, to put a few albums out.

"Fame is hard work," she said. "I'm overwhelmed just thinking about it."

We snorted crystal all through the night and Meme refreshed herself with several lines backstage in the studio restroom. She was given a scene to rehearse a few days before and she read it once and got the gist, she said. So much of her time had gone into playing the part of a famous actress she forgot to learn the part in the script, I guess. Backstage, she read the scene a second time, just minutes away from her turn. The script fluttered in her hand like a Japanese fan from all the methamphetamine flooding through her bloodstream.

It took her about ten seconds to perform the entire act, beginning to end. I remember Meme's mouth wide open and her lips twitching out a rush of bird calls, incoherent to everyone except herself. A hand dramatically thrown up in the air whipped downward and then crossed her abdomen to the other side. A leg was lifted in the air and remained there. The casting directors must have thought they were watching an original Kung Fu movie. The Oriental *dow* and *cow* sounds were cut off abruptly with a loud "Next!"

So much for making Herstory.

And to add to an already full blown life crisis, the day after her botched acting stint, Meme's poodle, Ralph, chased a pit bull in the park blocks. It took a lot longer than I expected for Ralph to realize the foolishness of this act. After a minute of being circled, spit-growled, and viciously glared at, the pit bull sank a couple fangs into the top part of Ralph's rear end. It was as if a sensitive button had been pushed to catapult Ralph out into the street, where he yelped one last time beneath the tire of a moving pick-up truck. Meme had a private burial service that I was forced to attend. Her mourning was bottomless.

Before the audition and Ralph's memorial, dramas reigned, but they were limited to pseudo-life-threatening episodes: a wet pillow; broken dishes; screams like apocalyptic trumpets. After the audition, the razor rituals made their debut. I think Meme interpreted my tender reaction to her suicide attempt as a great leap forward in the idle progress of our relationship.

I walk to the kitchen to look at some food. Look through the cupboards at the pasta and crackers, and then open the refrigerator—mostly empty. I haven't been able to eat all day and nothing here seems very appealing so I walk back and sit down and smoke another cigarette while I try to ignore the banging behind the bathroom door. I don't have to worry about Meme slitting her wrists in there. It's one of those things that she'll never do without an audience. But the noise grates on my nerves, and I know it won't end until I take back everything.

I walk to the bathroom to see what Meme is doing to herself. I push the door open and hang my head around the edge of the door to peek at the image of Meme in the mirror. Magazine clippings of Marilyn Monroe and Greta Garbo glitter at the edge of the mirror forming a cute, blonde frame.

Meme is darkening her eyes with black eyeliner. She leans forward like she is going to kiss the mirror, colors her lips a bright red and blows me a kiss instead.

"I'm sorry," I say, talking to the face in the mirror.

She picks up a round cosmetic case, opens it, powders the powder that's already on her face.

"Meme, please," I say, "we need to think this through."

"Right now," Meme says, applying more powder to the black circles under her eyes, "I just want to get high and not think about it at all."

I turn my head and blow cigarette smoke out of my mouth and look back at Meme through the mirror, over her shoulder, making eye contact as I'm about to kiss her on the back of the neck.

"I have arrived," Meme announces.

She blows herself a kiss.

"You are beautiful," I say, not mentioning how strung out she looked before she masked herself with make-up.

She winks at me and turns around. The white fur coat hangs slightly off each shoulder. Her breasts push through the silk slip and into my chest and my hands slide down her sides under the fur, down her hard ribs, down her slim waist.

"I know," she says, lifting her chin and nose toward the ceiling, "I'm beautiful."

"I know you know," I say, flicking some ash into the bathroom sink.

Meme walks out of the bathroom and hums to Billie Holiday. "Strange Fruit" is playing on the CD player. Meme stops in front of the life-size mirror and nods approvingly at her reflection. Billie Holiday sings her sorrow in the background.

"The bulging eyes and the twisted tongue," Meme sings along.

But it's not *tongue*. It's *mouth*. The twisted mouth of a black man after a lynching, hanging from a poplar tree, being plucked at by crows.

"You know," Meme says, holding a silver and black Versace dress in front of her body while she stares into the mirror, "when I listen to Billie Holiday sing I can feel the sorrow and pain of her life. She struggled to be somebody. I really identify with her."

Meme tosses the Versace dress onto the floor and then holds a white cotton voile slip dress in front of her, shaking her head no. I try to imagine Meme being denied a table at a restaurant or the use of a public restroom. I try to imagine Meme walking to the back of the bus. She holds the black Armani dress under her face and smiles. We won't have to run out and buy her a new dress today.

I sit on the chair and see nothing through the window. I think about Meme's suicide threats. Is she serious? Would it be such a bad thing? Suicide has been called the ultimate act of narcissism. Is that why Meme wants to kill herself? Because she loves herself too much? Do we always kill the thing we love? Is she staying with me to kill me because she loves me? Maybe she's right: maybe I would end up feeling like a murderer.

Meme strokes her red hair away from her face so it's held up behind her ears. She fiddles with her black purse, pulls out some powder, and whitens her white face. Meme puts the makeup away and watches herself sing the last stanza with Billie.

The white fur coat slips off Meme's shoulders, along with the white slip. The black dress covers the small bruises which crawl down her legs and across her bony body. She digs through some clothes on the floor.

"Oh! My! God!" Meme says, turning a suitcase upside down. "I left all my shoes at home." She throws thousand dollar dresses across the room. "I have to have my shoes!"

I'm wondering how far this is going to go.

"I can't live without my shoes!" she says, kicking a Gucci bag, knocking a box on its side. "We have to go get my shoes."

"We'll go get your shoes," I say. "We'll just drive up there. Okay? That's all we have to do." I flip my wrist in the air, flick ash on the floor, and take a drag. It's pretty fucking simple. "Okay?"

"Okay."

I'm driving Meme's white Volvo down Third Avenue. Meme lights up a cigarette and points out a couple of girls who are bumming for change. She thinks they are from The Hills and that they ran out of their allowance money.

"Look," she says.

A bag lady kicks a shopping cart, yells at it.

Meme laughs to herself.

Trash litters the streets. We drive slowly through down town, stopping at red lights. A couple of prostitutes wave. Meme waves back at them; we drive on. There are a lot of signs in this area that say "Drug Free Zone" and there is a guy sitting on the stairway of a closed-down restaurant, shooting up. A skinny old black man is standing on the street with his arms in the air, praising God, then his blistered and needle-tracked arms fall to his side.

"Is this a joke?" Meme asks. She coughs on the cigarette smoke and then pushes a button on the inside of the car door. The window glides down automatically. "What are these people living for?"

"Be nice," I tell her.

"Like you should talk," she says.

"Yeah?" I ask.

"Yeah," she says, "sure!"

I turn right on Burnside. More bums and junkies and young kids are walking down the sidewalks. You can hear people yelling and whistling at each other.

"Do you ever wonder why some people continue to live?" Meme asks.

"Human beings are masochists," I guess.

In the bright sunlight, Meme doesn't look so hot. Neither do I.

"Most people are nothing," she says and blows a ring of smoke.

Meme smiles, brushes her fingers through her dark red hair, and stares down on the streetwalkers.

"You know what I think about?" I ask. She turns her head to the side and looks at me. "I wonder what their dreams were when they were young."

We see a bum who is eating from a garbage can in front of a McDonald's. We stare at him while he extracts what looks like a smashed soda can and half a hamburger from the trash. He shoves the burger into his mouth. Some bread falls from his face and down to the ground. He bends over.

I look up and see a blue Volvo sign flashing. White-trash bars and traffic line up and down the street. Gas fumes mixed with the smell of fried mutated chicken from KFC's makes the air taste like grease. Meme takes a drag off her cigarette and the self-radiance disappears from her face. Her window closes automatically, softening the drone of the street traffic.

We leave it all behind and drive up a winding street into the Southwest Hills, passing beautiful houses with statues and manicured lawns. It takes about five minutes and we're in the money district. There are several cars in the driveway at her parents' house: a Mercedes; a BMW; and a Lexus that blocks the driveway so we can't park Meme's car in her old parking spot. She tells me to park behind it.

"Are you sure you want to go in?" I ask, turning the ignition off.

We are in no condition for family relations.

Chapter 2

▼

CAROL PORTER SERVICES (CPS)

One of my ads caught the attention of an entertainment scout, always on the lookout for novel ideas and bizarre kinks in nature. I've been curious all morning long—what would a showman want from me? I'm a therapist, not a juggler or a dwarf, not a cripple or a fire eater.

The entertainment executive, the man who created Bill Howard's Traveling Museum of Curiosities and Unbelievable Wonders, stands at about six and a half feet in my office doorway. A black custom-tailored tuxedo fits snugly around his chest and bulges out a good amount around his center. A soft red seems permanently blushed on his cheeks and pudgy nose. From the middle of his upper lip two thick, black waxy ropes of mustache stem out in opposite directions and curve upwards at their ends. A white ruffled shirt protrudes between the black velvet lapels of his tuxedo. His hair is black and greased apart down the middle.

He wraps his large warm hand firmly around mine and belts out in a startling operatic voice, "I'm Mr. Bill Howard! Pleased to meet ya!"

"I'm Carol," I say.

He lets go of my hand and I secretly recover from a loss of breath, a skipped heartbeat, a jolted equilibrium all induced by the carnival barker's howl.

"Please sit down," I say, sweeping my hand toward the chair.

He strolls across the office, quietly clicking his black patent leather shoes, slips a hand into the inside pocket of his tuxedo and pulls a dark brown jumbo cigar out from under the soft velvet lapel. His large egg-shaped body squeezes into the chair. His stomach rolls. A meaty hand stubs out from a white cuff and flicks a gold-cased lighter, torching a tall flame through the end of the cigar. He puffs multiple clouds of smoke.

"Portland is a quaint little metropolis," Mr. Howard pets his mustache. "I don't think I've been through here before. Kind of boring. Not much going on. A little out of touch with the real world. But it's got a ripeness to it. Like it's waiting for something to happen."

"It's a decent town," I say. "I've thought about moving somewhere bigger. But I do okay here."

"But you could always do much better!" Mr. Howard says. He holds the cigar to his mouth and takes a puff. "Carol, it is a big wonder that I chanced upon the tiny advertisement for your eccentric services. And the footnote about your self-published self-help book only caught the printer's attention, I bet. How many copies have you sold?"

None. I don't say this. I say nothing.

"That's what I thought," Mr. Howard says. "You need to think larger than life. Advertising is everything. If you don't have publicity, you don't have a show. That's the way I figure. And you need an attractive arrangement of sorts." Mr. Howard gestures toward the emptiness of my office with his smoky cigar. "Kind of like what those Catholics got going with all that divine architecture surrounding a little confessional. American lives are stocked full of poorly-crafted relics and decapitated landscapes. What they want is a spiritual transportation from their vulgar boredom to something majestically supernatural. Something to make the blood jet about in their bodies. This office inspires like a pitch-black dust-laden attic." Mr. Howard sighs in discontent. "I don't see a single amusement in this entire office!"

I contemplate the adequacy of my office. A chair for myself and another for a client. A yellow upholstered vinyl couch for naps. A small bookshelf with a dozen copies of my book, *The Pigs' Hammer: Preying on Sexual Predators*, lined vertically across. A plaque behind my desk that reads:

CERTIFICATE
OF THE
ONE HUNDRED MINUTE SEMINAR
Awarded to
CAROL PORTER

"What's this got to do with me?" I ask, tapping my finger on my temple. "I'm a counselor, I'm a therapist. I treat people and their mental illnesses."

Mr. Howard swipes the top of the gold lighter with his hand and a two or three inch yellow flame is sucked into the end of his brown cigar. The corner of his mouth opens, releasing white balls of smoke that drift up and thin to gray.

"I want to make a deal," Mr. Howard says. "You say in your ad that you can help people remember that they were Cleopatra in their past lives? Or that they were Joan of Arc or Napoleon?" Mr. Howard pulls my ad out of his tan leather briefcase. "You say you can take a normal person with a normal past and help her remember numerous affairs with death, ungodly abuse while in the fallopian tube, and saddening memories of incest by a father she has always worshipped and adored? Survivors of brutal Satanic rituals! Women with dozens of personalities! They switch and talk differently?" He looks up at me from the ad, trading hands with the ad and cigar. "I would like to meet one of these women inflicted with multiple personalities. A survivor of a virginal sacrifice! A lady with horrifying prenatal memories! And if I like what I see, I would like to have her on Reality TV. If that's a hit, then maybe have her exhibited for an entire season in my traveling museum."

I stand up and figuratively show Mr. Howard to the door by walking over and opening it.

"Mr. Howard," I say, "I belong to a respectable profession. This is a place for therapy and healing with the clients' interests at heart. Therefore, I have no interest in whatever scam you have devised for the sake of profit. It would be irresponsible to even give it consideration. Goodbye."

Mr. Howard pushes his round body out of the chair, puffs the brown cigar like a train steam engine, and sways his arrogance toward me. He flicks invisible lint off his cuff, extends his hand with the cigar until it rests on the door, then pushes it shut.

"Carol," Mr. Howard says, purposefully discarding ash onto my floor. "Let's face the facts. Counselors like you are a dime a dozen. All you need to be a therapist these days is a plaque obtained from some bogus seminar and a faint familiarity with the ABCs. I've been in show business for a long time and I've got a good eye for golden opportunities like this."

Mr. Howard's large hand holds my shoulder and gently guides me back toward my desk. The waxed mustache rises and shines in front of his red cheeks while he talks.

"This is a once-in-a-lifetime offering," Mr. Howard says. "Once the new thing is done, it is done. My greatest attractions burned out after a few years, internationally. Locally, the new thing becomes yesterday's news in no time."

I'm slumping back down into my chair, looking up at Mr. Howard standing above me in front of my desk.

"This little gig you've got going with Multiple Personality Disorder and Repressed Memory Syndrome is loaded with potential. It is sensational, I love it, don't get me wrong, but it's just another amusement, like Bon Jovi wearing spandex, to get people through the night. A trend that will end with the next new thing. I'm making you an offer to take your show on the road. I will make a mint and so will you—that is, of course, if you oblige while the going's good." Mr. Howard sticks the wet brown stub of his cigar into the side of his mouth. "I can find some other psychologist with a Freudian crystal ball and a counterfeit certificate indicating intelligence, if you like." He blows the cigar smoke over my desk where it hovers like the black cloud over my life and says, "And you'll miss out on a fortune."

Most of my clients commit suicide or get hauled off to the mental institution. Either way, it's bad for business. I've got my regular appointments. Frustrated housewives. Pipe-dreamers working at convenience stores and gas stations. Others who come once or twice and never return. Then there is the support group. Ten women and their multiple personalities competing to share their stories. Who has the most sick and twisted memory tonight?

Things got out of control after I introduced my clients to the idea of Satanic ritual abuse. Since then, the support group has been all about Satanic bestiality and slaughter. I made the suggestion to a client one day while she was under hypnosis. She brought it up during a support group session and it spread like wildfire. By the end of the session I had ten Satanic priestesses for clients and they all described in vivid detail their escape from a virginal sacrifice. After I watched a science fiction movie about an extraterrestrial, I raised the question about alien abductions while a client was under the clock. This had a more devastating effect on another support group session. I'm not making enough money to baby-sit ten neurotic women while they slam out stories about a sexually obsessed E.T. and his nasty finger.

It's not that I think the repressed memories are true or false. After all, there's a little bit of truth to everything. And a little bit that is false. What matters is that my clients have some serious problems. Repressed Memory Syndrome and Multiple Personality Disorder are rather satisfying manifestations of the internal nightmare they are experiencing. Maybe a client hasn't actually endured scarification at the hands of a Satanic Cult, but for all the neglect and loneliness of childhood this memory of ritualistic hell is an apt representation for the suffering and ostracism she was dealt from life's wicked deck of cards. I want my clients to express their feelings, speak out, take back the night and all that, even if they have to play around with metaphors and stretch the truth a great deal. It's their healing that matters.

But as the chronicler of their mental ordeals, I should be making a lot more money than I am.

Every week a client's insurance coverage is pulled out from underneath me. Another client will off herself. Someone else gets transferred to the mental ward. I'm trying to build up a consistent clientele. I need my clients to always come back for more. Business is business—something Mr. Howard knows a lot about.

"How much time do I have to make a decision?" I ask.

Mr. Howard consults the gold Rolex on his right wrist.

"You have until the end of this meeting," Mr. Howard says, contemplatively twisting one side of his long black mustache. "Time is money."

Certain images play in my mind: Mr. Howard arriving in a Rolls Royce. The driver opening the door, Mr. Howard rolling confidently onto the sidewalk. The look of embarrassment when he confirms the address is correct on the hideous building where my office resides. The manner in which he has unsuccessfully attempted to tolerate the unprofessional atmosphere of my office. At times straining hopelessly, it seems, to sustain the belief that this business proposition is a smart one.

"How much are you offering?"

"For you and a client with multiple personalities on Reality TV," Mr. Howard says, "$25000, and you get to advertise your book. If this is as big as I think it's going to be, I'll double that figure for a seasonal exhibition in my mobile museum. You can continue to practice your therapy sessions between shows. If that's a success, I say we go international! London! Paris! Rome! All you have to do is make your clients and sessions available at my discretion. I'll even set you up in an office designed according to the laws of popular aesthetics, furnishings included. You can go about your business as usual, only in an atmosphere conducive to the rigorous standards of your profound services. Just think of me as a deliverer of your talent and message to the world at large."

Reality TV would be perfect for the display of my clients' suppressed emotions. This would give them an audience to witness their stories and validate their feelings. I can market my book with state-of-the-art advertising in exchange for his public relations skills. I can have a real office with a Freudian chaise longue and Oriental rugs.

"After all this hits the big time," Mr. Howard says, "you'll be the guest of Kings and Queens! The talk of Hollywood celebrities and socialites! Perhaps an invitation to entertain the White House staff! It's either you or someone else. You decide. Do we have a deal?"

I lean over my desk and extend my hand.

"It's a deal."

Mr. Howard introduces me to his road trip TV crew. A man seven or eight feet tall, with a bulky black TV camera exposing wires down his shoulders, ducks his way into my office.

"This is Pinhead," Mr. Howard says, "my cinematographer extraordinaire."

I squint upward at Pinhead while he bends forward and down with the zoom lens coiling in and out near my face. His long arm strikes out three or four feet and pets my hand, then a head the size of a small cantaloupe pokes out from the side of the black camera.

"I'm Pinhead," he says with a high pitched squeaky voice, his mouth dilated like a terrified monkey's.

I remove my hand from his creepy caress, stuttering, "I'm…Carol," as a midget in a black tuxedo walks between Pinhead's legs.

"And this is Stump," Mr. Howard says. "He's in charge of lighting. Don't worry, we have plenty of ladders."

Stump's gray afro defies gravity, extending beyond his reach above his scalp. He holds out his short disjointed arm and grabs part of my hand, wrapping all his fingers around two of mine.

"Nice to meet you, Stump," I say.

He nods dramatically and silently shakes my hand.

I make some phone calls to try to get all my clients together for an interview with Mr. Howard. I manage to contact six of them. Whether or not they'll show, that's the question. This is never an easy task. Pulled in different directions by competitive personalities, a client will be on her way to my office and then later snap out of a blackout while she's standing in a crowd at a concert or in the middle of a bar fight somewhere. The excuses vary. One night the hooker side takes over and I have to bail a client out of jail. Other times I just hope a client is fabricating the details of a killing spree. Tall-tales as part of the healing process kind of thing. A narrative for the current state of her psyche. The client is giving me a sign to interpret. Reality is subjective anyway.

Other clients have other problems. First, all my clients lose their jobs immediately following the first session. Shortly thereafter they end their marriages and break off all relations with their parents. It's all part of the healing process. One has to go through a lot of shit before one can get better.

Some of them don't even make it that far. One client can't make it today because she drank a gallon of gasoline and then licked the tip of a burning match. She had so much inner turmoil, she ultimately exploded into a blazing rage of fire.

She left a suicide note:

I have lost everything.
My life is getting worse and worse.
I can't go on any longer.

What a shame. She was my first client. A real soldier.

Other clients get to where they can't get out of bed anymore. They lay there all day rehashing memories of childhood abuse they learned about under hypnosis. Quaking with body memories when the memory is too vivid and strong. They gag and choke from the thought of particular sexual acts. Others lay about in a comatose state from the pill cocktails prescribed to take the edge off the hallucinations of Satanic ritual abuse and alien abductions.

Pinhead and Stump set up the TV equipment while we wait for the clients to arrive. Pinhead folds out a ladder to the side of my desk, Stump crawls one step at a time to the top and waits for someone to hand him the lights. Pinhead walks around the office, pushing various buttons on the abstract filming device, his face completely hidden.

Mr. Howard wants me to show him everything I've got, the inside and out of my trade. The operations of my eccentric services.

"These are the staple symptoms for Multiple Personality Disorder," I say. "I look for people with family problems and suicidal tendencies. Drug abusers. Failures in general. According to the seminar, Multiple Personality Disorder is caused by trauma in early life. What happens is the trauma is so traumatic it must be repressed for the individual's survival and then stored in another personality.

This suppression results in the individual's failure to lead a life of accomplishment and prosperity. That's when I come in. The repressed memories must be unearthed and confronted for one to become whole again. My favorite technique is called reenactment. When the client reenacts the abuse a more vivid recall tends to follow. Ultimately the client becomes familiar with all of her personalities and develops relationships with them. Ideally, we would want all the personalities to become friends with the victim. But they can be finicky and impossible at times. Valium helps with that."

Mr. Howard stretches out a stem of black mustache, nodding his head. Pinhead clanks a silver-shelled light on a swivel at the top of the ladder. Stump pivots the light while Pinhead plugs the cord into a circuit in the wall.

"Depression is a favorite among my clients," I say. "Prozac is highly recommended as a temporary cure for bouts of despair, frustration, and your typical run-of-the-mill existential blues. Most of my clients down anti-depressants like candy. A favorite for kids is Ritalin. Parents just love this one because Ritalin does the parenting all by itself!"

One stem of the black mustache springs up into a curl when released from Mr. Howard's fingertips.

"Nice touch!" Mr. Howard bellows. "Medication makes the healing process remotely scientific. It has a ring of credibility to it!"

I pull a Sex Victim Kit out of my desk drawer and open it.

Mr. Howard sticks a cigar in his mouth and chews on the tobacco leaf, his yellow teeth showing where the lip is curled up on one side. The lighter clicks out a flame. He puffs quietly, exhaling while he looks up at the video cassette in my hand.

"This is a classic, the movie *Sybil*," I say. "If I ever had an assistant to my practice, this is it. A client comes in, confused, I inform her that her failures are a result of repressed memories. Unknown abuse suffered in early childhood. She doesn't know what to think or how to act. After a single viewing of *Sybil*, she's got the splitting and switching personalities thing down to a T."

I dig around in the Sex Victim Kit and pull out a couple of trophies.

"Where would we be without hope?" I ask. "Without the vision of green pastures on the other side of the horizon? Most of my clients want to be somebody special. They have dreams about becoming a famous actress or a Rock 'n' Roll star sweating on the stage and pulsating from the vibrations of the roar of praise. Every woman secretly wants to be Madonna or the reincarnation of Greta Garbo. That's why I throw in the plastic gold painted Oscar trophy and the tin Golden

Globe award. Something to aspire towards. Something to focus on, to believe in. To make them think their trials and tribulations will all add up to something."

"You've got a little showman's blood in ya, after all!" Mr. Howard says, pointing his cigar at me accusingly.

I pull a copy of my self-help book from the shelf and hand it to Mr. Howard. He sits on the opposite side of my desk, skimming the contents of *The Pigs' Hammer*.

Stump turns the light on and rotates it without coordination, spotlighting the floor and the ceiling. Pinhead's camera stares at me like a one-eyed robot. The lens buzzes like a bee, moves in and out. I sit upright in my chair with an air of professionalism.

"'The Checklist' is voluminous!" Mr. Howard howls. "It nearly diagnoses all living creatures as sex abuse victims!"

"It's better to be safe than sorry," I say.

"It's something everyone can identify with!" Mr. Howard says.

"Repressed Memory Syndrome is a common phenomenon," I say.

"We'll have everyone's attention!" Mr. Howard says victoriously. He lifts the book above his head. "Every broken family in America will have it sitting on their night stand! Our show will put TV evangelism to shame!"

The six clients file into the office, babbling like children on the floor. Someone is speaking in tongues. Stump shakes nervously at the top of the ladder while a couple clients plead to hold him like a stuffed animal. Pinhead zooms in and out with his camera so the women keep a cautious distance. Mr. Howard is looking over my clients disdainfully.

"Mr. Howard would like to meet each and everyone of you," I say. "Quiet, please listen up, hush. Pay attention please. Leave Stump alone. Mr. Howard would like to hear all of your stories and get to know some of your personalities. Who would like to go first?"

It's like watching a bunch of children fistfight in a sandbox.

"Michelle," I say, "you can go first. Everybody else wait outside my office. I'll call you when it's your turn."

Mr. Howard takes the seat behind my desk and I have Michelle sit in the chair in front of him. Michelle's black hair hangs down over her hollow cheeks. Her weight has dropped to eighty pounds since I diagnosed her as an anorexic.

Pinhead positions himself above Mr. Howard's shoulder and Stump casts the light into Michelle's eyes. I tell her to tell Mr. Howard about herself. She pushes both hands into her crotch and holds them there.

"My name is Michele Agatha and I have fifteen personalities and I was molested by my dad and he's in prison now and I was a priestess in a Satanic Cult and they made me do horrible things…"

"Cut," Mr. Howard says, breaking off a new cigar. "Too timid. Too frail. We need spunk! Liveliness! Someone who'll stand out in the crowd and not fall away into the shadows!"

Michelle lowers her head into her lap and cries into her hands. Pinhead resets the camera and I lead Michelle outside and bring Bozanne back in with me. At 499 pounds, she's kind of hard to miss.

Bozanne is too big for the chair so she spreads herself out on the yellow vinyl couch. She sulks into her layers of protection, rotates her big rusty tractor of a head in my direction, looks into my eyes. I extend a hand which she clasps in hers, pressing her dry sausage-plump fingers into my palm. I tell her to share her story with Mr. Howard.

Pinhead attempts to fit Bozanne's body into a single frame. He stands tall in the corner for a crane shot. The lens buzzes tiredly from the farthest part of the room near the window. He finally settles on a close-up from that position.

"I know it's hard," I say, "but you can do it."

Bozanne clinches my hand and tears roll down her mountainous arms like lava. She coughs, gathers herself together, resting her arms and hands on her belly—just a little below her third chin. Pinhead's camera buzzes from the corner.

"My name is Bozanne and I have forty-two personalities—a group record—and I was molested by my father and all of his friends and my aunts and uncles and my grandma and grandpas."

She pulls her head up, then dips it down, grunting. Stump lights her face up. Bozanne's black scraggly hair hasn't been washed for weeks because her arms are too heavy to lift that high. She opens the plastic wrapping of a Twinkie and continues with white filling on her lips:

"And I was raped by the Pope and I was a priestess in the Satanic Cult until Carol saved me," she takes a big breath, expanding like a balloon the size of a blimp, "and I have been in the group for a year and so far I've lost one pound and in my past lives I was an Apache and a Negro brought to America through the slave trade. That's why I eat so many Twinkies!"

Bozanne raises her sliced up arms midway in the air with the flab sagging back down on her stomach.

"I must be getting a lot better," she says, peeling a bandage off her left wrist to reveal a fresh razor cut. "Look!"

Mr. Howard looks at me, confused. He shrugs his cigar.

"Razor cuts symbolize rank around here," I say. "They kind of denote status among the group. The more slits you've got trailing up and down your arm, the longer you've been in therapy."

Mr. Howard takes a slow drag off the cigar, lets the smoke leave his mouth on its own.

"That's brilliant!" Mr. Howard barks. "A woman the size of a rhinoceros violently slashing her wrists like a delirious swordsman! But this still isn't big enough! Maybe something to show between the second and third act."

Mr. Howard dismisses Bozanne with his cigar and she wobbles her way across the floor and out the door of my office.

We audition the four remaining clients. Some are good enough for sideshows, Mr. Howard says, objects to fill up intermissions. But none of them fit the bill for Howard-style stardom. Pinhead helps Stump down the ladder and removes the light from its swivel. Mr. Howard strolls across the room to the office window and turns around. He pulls the cigar out of his mouth and looks at me through a cloud of cigar smoke.

"Let me tell you a story about Albert Little." Mr. Howard orchestrates his cigar with each word. "Albert Little was a freak of nature, no doubt, like many of your clients. He was a midget, although I advertised him as a dwarf. He was four years old, though I advertised him as being twelve. Anyhow, that makes no difference. He was a midget and therefore suffered an unfortunate abnormality. But the difference between Albert Little and the other midgets was his charm and elegance in manner. His body was proportionate, no deformity whatsoever. He was a little man who was pleasing to the eye. Then I would add my Midas touch. I would dress him up like a gladiator and the Queen of England would go ape shit crazy. I would strip him naked and have him posing on the stage like a Samson and people would pull out all their hair and faint. Now, your clients are abundantly supplied with abnormalities. They have their little tragedies. These things are definitely integral to show business. But we need to deliver something that is cathartic and blissful for The Mundane. They deserve a little pleasure now and then, you know. We need to entertain if we want to compete with the stylized news teams that model world news segments after sitcoms and Broadway productions. Who wants to sit through sixty minutes about the Two Towers without Beethoven's 9th playing in the background?" Mr. Howard blows on the end of his cigar, turning the ash into a bright red. "So what we need to do is take this tragedy of recovered memories of childhood abuse, these tales of Satanic rituals and alien abduction, and publicly document them. We need to make the abnormality electrifying, like I did with Albert Little, to hold on to the attention deficit society. Sadly, none of your clients have the potential to be the Reality TV prize I am looking for."

I feel like I've misplaced a winning lottery ticket. A confrontation with all of my empty wishes. Teased. To be forever tantalized by some other counselor Mr. Howard will tuck under his wing while I sit in front of the TV or the big screen thinking to myself, that could have been me. If only a few other clients would have shown up. If only I hadn't buried the rest.

"How long are you going to be in town?" I ask.

"I'll be leaving tomorrow afternoon," he says, lifting his leather briefcase, holding out a hand. "If you come up with anyone by then, give me a call. I hate to leave empty handed."

I hold his hand with my sweat-filled palm.

"I will," I say confidently. "Believe me, I will."

I have three remaining possibilities. One client who hasn't left her bed for the last two weeks, not even to go to the bathroom. Another client who won't get off the couch in front of the TV to answer my phone calls. Another one who has traded her meds back in for her old heroin addiction.

What I need right now is a miracle.

CHAPTER 3
▼

THE DYSFUNCTIONAL FAMILY

Meme jingles the silver bracelets on her wrist with a motion for me to be quiet—she wants to get in and out of the house without a confrontation with her parents. From the living room we can hear people talking in the courtyard out back. Through a large bay window I see Meme's grandma and grandpa talking with her parents while they stand around the flower garden and fountains. Her little brother and sister pick at the hors d'oeuvres on the long white clothed table that holds other dishes piled with orange lobsters, burgundy meats, sliced breads, round cheeses, a silver bucket filled with ice and a green bottle of champagne.

Meme tells me again to be quiet. She looks at herself in the Victorian mirror in the hallway. I remember the way it used to be, in Meme's flesh. The night Meme obliterated her hopes of Hollywood stardom with that embarrassing demonstration of tribal performance art, she shattered the mirror and tried to use the broken glass to cut herself. The glass cut too clumsily so she pulled out the razor from her drug pouch. We were both tripping hard from a row of days laced with insomnia and speed and the culmination of Meme's shipwrecked dream. There was blood everywhere and the only thing I really remember about that night is Meme crying for what seemed to be forever and telling me she would rather die than be a loser. A failure. Mediocre. It was a bad night and we got the mirror fixed and the oriental rugs on the hardwood floors cleaned before her parents returned from a vacation in Paris. We charged it to her father's credit card.

Meme straightens the mirror; it almost falls off the wall, but she gets a hold of it. She then makes a sign with her finger to tell me she'll be back in a minute. I wait, standing in the hall, motionless and quiet. I hear Meme turning things upside down in her father's study just below the stairs; mumbled voices carry from the courtyard. I pace around the dining room, repeatedly glancing at the back door in case somebody comes in. Meme eventually steps out of the study and lifts up a hand, waves a couple hundred dollar bills in my face. She shoves the money in her cleavage under the Armani dress, then smiles and turns to walk up the stairs to get her shoes.

Meme's younger sister, Jill, walks through the back door and skips across the kitchen floor in a violet dress with white daisy prints. Two blonde pony-tails swing behind her head.

"Meme!" Jill yells.

The conversation out back reduces to whispers.

"Oh God," Meme says.

"Meme," Jill stops at the bottom of the stairs, "are you really moving out for good?"

"I'm not here," Meme says. "Okay? You don't see me."

"Grandma and grandpa are here," Jill says.

Meme turns to go upstairs.

"I have to get my shoes," she says.

Meme's father walks in, decked out in black tie and windblown hair that Meme has no doubt helped thin and gray. He looks at me with his head tilted back with eyes split in two by the line of bifocals. He places his champagne flute down on the Chippendale dining room table, cups his chin with a hand, slides it down to his bow tie.

"Hello," he says in a dry, dead voice. "How you doing, Frank?"

I put my jittery hands in my pants pockets and try to avoid eye contact.

"Good," I say.

His presence makes me self-conscious. I wonder if he knows that I'm only a passive accomplice to Meme's little schemes. When Meme threw a party and served that case of twenty year old vintage French wine, that was her idea. And of course I was going to try it. But the check and Visa card forgeries and his dead grandmother's box of jewelry, that was Meme's singular doing. I even tried to dissuade her, I swear I did. He must know by now the sure impossibility of sidetracking Meme when she sets her mind to something, especially if it's a family taboo.

Meme's father folds his arms across his pouching stomach.

"How are you, Meme?" he asks.

Meme steps down a step with one leg, shifting her hip out to one side where a hand rests on her upper ass in fuck-you fashion.

"Very good, thank you."

She looks back at him with bloodshot eyes. Meme looks so pale, almost looks dead, and I wonder how strung out I look right now. I wonder what her father is thinking. What it means to be Meme's father.

"Do you want me to get you something to drink?" he asks. "You look like you need to eat something."

"We're just stopping by," Meme says. She turns her head away from her father and stares at the wall lined with black and white family portraits to the side of the stairwell. "I stopped by to get my shoes."

"Why don't you say hello to your grandparents," her father says, "and have some dinner?"

"We are kind of in a hurry," Meme says, twisting the strap on her purse around her fingers. "I don't really feel like it right now."

"You look strung out again," he says quietly, glancing at me. He holds his hands together in front of his chest and says, "Why don't you guys give rehab a try? Get some help."

Meme's father and I had a bonding experience that to this very day haunts me every time I see him. This happened after one of Meme's accidental near-death experiences. Meme and I were at the Polis Club with our friends Paul and Amber. Meme had left for the restroom and was missing for a while. I found her staggering against the wall in the hallway outside the restroom area with white powder on her nose and lips. She was already so high and then she finished off enough crystal to take just about anyone for a week-long ride. Sounds, voices, unrecognizable ballads reverberated in the hallway where Meme was leaning against a wall and compulsively rocking her head. She was rapidly twirling her hair around her fingers and holding the white fur coat over her breasts like a blanket. Sweat drops soaked her entire face and blood ran down from her nose, circled her mouth, and continued down her chin while she mumbled about the stains on her fur coat.

I led her to the restroom and frantically splashed handfuls of water at her face and coat, diluting the blood to a soft pink that sprinkled all over the yellow octagonal tiles on the restroom floor. Paul and Amber found us there and Amber ran off to call 911. Paul reeled toilet paper off the dispenser and kept telling Meme she was going to be okay, everything is okay, but the wadded toilet paper stuck up her nose couldn't hold back the flow of blood that painted her neck red and soaked her black dress. Meme stumbled out of the restroom and Paul and I followed her out to the sidewalk in front of the club where she fell, pounding her body up and down on the concrete sidewalk. Strands of blood-clumped hair stuck to the front of her fur coat and vomit and blood bubbled out of her mouth. I kept thinking about how much speed was flowing through Meme's veins and what a horrible way to die.

Hours seemed to go by but it was only minutes later that an ambulance showed up, the paramedics pushed the crowd away, and placed what I thought was a corpse on the stretcher. They let me go along with her and the sirens sounded as the ambulance drove to the nearest hospital. I held Meme's lifeless hand in mine.

They had already pumped Meme's stomach by the time her father showed up around two in the morning. Her father stood at Meme's hospital bedside in black slacks and a red pinstriped pajama top. Meme seemed breathless under the white and blue oxygen mask that covered her face. Her father held her hand to his lips and cried. He petted the hair on her head where wires were suctioned to her temples. His eyes drifted back and forth between Meme and her life support system.

In the waiting room not a word was said until we received official news that Meme was going to be alright. Then we had a man-to-man talk about cleaning up the self-destructive act Meme and I had been putting on. Meme's father suggested we both check into rehab and I told him that it sounded like a good idea. He suggested that we both go down to the university and apply to college and I told him it was on the agenda for things to do tomorrow.

The next day, after Meme got out of the hospital, we recuperated for a few hours, watched TV and got bored and depressed until Geber supplied us with a few bags of heavenly ecstasy. All that talk about going straight was just nervous air, but her father keeps at it anyway and never mentions the word 'rehab' in my presence without looking me straight in the eye.

Meme's pale green face is bent down, mostly hidden behind a head of greasy red hair. I turn away and see her stepmother walking into the kitchen. She's wearing a Florentine dress with large bananas, pineapples and lemons on it. Giant pearls ring her neck in three long strands. Her red hair is pulled back, slicked tight, and she looks exactly like Meme, maybe a year younger. She tightens her face, walks into the room and stands with her ivory bracelets crossed over her arms.

Meme's younger sister is the one who told us that her stepmother refers to us as The Thieves. The disappearance of Meme's dead great grandmother's jewelry box earned us this title for good. I get the feeling that if she had it her way, Meme would have been arrested a long time ago. But her father wants to avoid that kind of situation; a criminal record could mar future opportunities and make a clean slate less appealing. Meanwhile, Meme wreaks havoc on their lives, upsets their bank accounts, hocks priceless household fixtures, and does everything else just short of destroying her parents' marriage, which is always more at odds when Meme is around.

George sips his champagne. It is so quiet I can hear him swallow. He lifts a hand up to the knot of the black silk bow tie, loosens it, then unbuttons the top button of his pressed, white cotton shirt. He sighs softly and turns to me, then looks at his wife.

I'm becoming paranoid about looking paranoid.

Meme turns away from her father and focuses her attention on her hair, petting the red strands hanging in front of her shoulder with her fingers.

"We really need to get going," Meme says.

"Meme," he says, "I want to talk to you...just for a minute."

Meme pretends not to hear him. His hands and face develop a twitch while he tries to think of something to say. He removes his tuxedo jacket.

"Meme!" he says, placing his jacket on the dining room table.

Meme sighs and stumbles on the runner that layers the stairs.

"We can talk later."

"You should at least meet with your grandparents."

"I'll meet with them the next time," Meme sings out.

She hums something to herself and pretends to be bored while her face turns whiter. Meme frees herself from the rug and continues up the stairs, the curves of her bare ass showing through the tight black Armani dress.

"Meme, please," her father says.

I can hear Meme's footsteps as she runs upstairs. George stares at me. I'm too tired to move. I can't even see his eyes through the cloud in my head. But I can feel him looking at me like this is my piece of work. His daughter. This stray bitch with an attitude that keeps sniffing out my life. I turn my back on him. My way of saying, *don't look at me, she was your project for eighteen years!*

George walks past me. His pressed shirt is wrinkled and wet with sweat near his armpits. He steps into his study, comes out, and quickly walks up the spiral staircase.

"Meme!" he says.

I wait near the front door where I look out the window at the panoramic view of the city that looks like a computerized graphic. An unreal image. Everything looks so fake and staged from a distance.

I can hear Meme and her father stomping around upstairs, arguing about whether or not Meme needs to seek some kind of help or treatment. They talk about stolen checks and money. Meme says she has no idea what he is talking about.

"Maybe *you* should seek some help," Meme says, thumping back down the stairs ahead of her father.

"I'm trying to help you," her father says.

"Help *yourself*," she says.

To be honest, I don't know what all the fuss is about. He's getting a good deal here. The Fury is abandoning his home and he's acting like she's cauterizing off the legs he stands on by doing so. Sure, parental love is a morally upright and biological affair, but you have to draw the line somewhere.

Meme's grandparents appear in the living room, staring the way old people do when they think of the future. Her grandmother gently touches the large white hoop earring that hangs off her ear and says to Meme's stepmother, "Is she *stoned* again?"

Her stepmother says something about how Meme does things like this on purpose to be the center of attention. Meme slowly struts down the hall, beauty pageant style, with a big Gucci bag full of shoes and tries to reach for the door knob through my stomach.

"Meme," I say, blocking the door with my body, "maybe you should stay and work this out."

Meme slaps her forehead, jingling her bracelets, and waves her hand above her head.

"Have you lost it?" She holds her mouth open. Her thick lips form a grotesque red square. "This is not your problem!"

Now, it is my problem. But I don't say that. Because this could get ugly. Meme, I could say, you are impossible to live with. Please, go back up to your bedroom and be the plague to your family if you must. I beg you, please leave me out of it.

George walks down the hall toward us, his black leather shoes tapping all over the hardwood floors. I give him my *I cannot live with your daughter; please save me from her* look. Meme's mother gives me a *you made your bed, now sleep in it* look. Over her shoulder I see the silhouette of Meme's grandparents. They are so old they don't have any features, just thick skin on their faces.

"I think she's *stoned*," her grandmother nods.

"Meme, please," her father says.

Meme digs her fingernails into my arm and lowers me to the floor. She struts past with the Gucci bag hauled on her shoulder and says, "Fuck all of you!"

Her father asks if I'm okay as I follow Meme to the car.

I get in the driver's seat and smile. I just don't think things can get any worse. There's some security in this realization. All I have to do is play this out, and eventually something good will happen to me. The law of probability will make it so.

"I don't want to hear another word from you," Meme says, sitting in the passenger seat of the car, digging through the Gucci bag for the right pair of shoes.

I start the car and pull out of the driveway. Meme flings shoes over her shoulder to the back seat, really over-exerting herself in her search for the right pair. Fashion is Meme's idea of a workout.

She reaches for the cell phone, a hand still sunk in her shoe collection, and dials a number.

"What are you doing?" I ask her.

"I'm calling Geber," she says, slamming a shoe out the window.

Meme finally settles for a pair of plain black shoes and impatiently waits for something to happen on the other end of the line. A few seconds pass by quietly. Then she talks to the phone. A smile forms on her mouth; life enters into her body.

A song called "So What" rings through the Polis Club. Meme and I are sitting on a couple of black velvet chairs. I pull out a couple cigarettes and give one to Meme. She puts it in her mouth, leans forward, and I light her cigarette before mine. We stare out at the dance floor where the lights blink on and off, reflecting wet skin. She gets up and motions one finger in the air telling me she will be right back and I watch her slither in a white fur coat and disappear out of my view.

Amber's bleached-blonde head and red velvet jacket flow through a crowd.

The music speaker is made to look like the tortured face of Jesus with the fake thorns and blood and the words "So What" come out of Jesus' mouth. Out on the dance floor one man is jolting with his body wrapped in chains and another woman wears a white wedding dress and wings her arms cautiously like a wind-up ballerina doll under the strobe light. A couple of boys with leather bondage gear strapped over their chests and faces, collars around their necks, each hooked to the other by a chain, lounge out on a Victorian couch on the other side of the dance floor. A little kid who is in a dark corner, his shaved head bent down, bobs to the bass of the music. He moves his hands in front of his face to watch the tracers; he looks like he is about ten years old. Meme approaches me from out of nowhere and yells something I cannot understand. She leans closer.

"Geber is downstairs," she says, pointing her finger down at the floor.

"I saw Amber head down there," I say loudly, in competition with the Industrial rage.

Meme perks her lips, takes my hand, pulls me up from the chair and we walk toward the stairway and down the stairs, through two large black doors, and down the hallway, passing about ten people who are waiting in line to use the restroom. Paul and Amber are at the front of the line with Geber.

We all nod and Meme says something in Geber's ear, but the music is so loud I can't hear the exact words. Geber nods again. His head is badly shaved with scrapes all over it. Meme looks at me, her eyes light up. Her chin dimples.

"What do you have?" I mouth to Geber.

"The elixir of potential," he says in his jagged voice. He forms a smile out of the sores around his mouth. "Such stuff as dreams are made on."

Meme unfolds two one hundred dollar bills and hands them to Geber. He reaches into his army-green jacket, pulls out a tin case, opens it, shuffles around the little plastic bags of crystal meth and then hands her about eight of them. He assures us that it is very, *very* good. Meme eagerly knocks on the restroom doors. One of them is open and Geber nods at us and says he'll see us later.

We all walk into the restroom. My shoes squish into the floor. The wall may stain my hand if I reach out and touch it.

"It reeks in here," Meme says.

She shuts the door behind her. Paul and Amber collect money from their pockets to give to Meme.

"Look at this place," Meme says, irritable under the yellow lights. "This is a fucking dive, look at the toilet seat, it's yellow, the floor is yellow. Where do these people come from who pee on the floor?"

Meme pulls out her drug pouch and rests the mirror and a razor on the top of the toilet paper dispenser. She empties three little bags and whitens the mirror with powder, cautiously cuts it, slices the little pile into lines and then into a pile again and then into two lines. Her red hair swings over her right shoulder with one flip of the head; she leans down on the dispenser, and her face contorts while she drags the straw over a white line. She tilts her head up and her face blushes. For the next few seconds her entire life is focused on inhaling through her right nostril.

Amber and Paul cut their lines on the porcelain sink.

Meme hands me the straw and I hunch down and finish a line while she fills an eye-dropper with water and squirts up her nostril to get all the crystal down.

"This place is a hole," Meme says, putting the mirror and razor back in the pouch and in her purse. "A hole!"

Someone bangs on the restroom door, says, "Hurry up in there."

"I don't know," Paul says.

"Something's not right," Amber says.

"This junk is cut with shit," Meme says. "That's what I think."

My nostrils burn clear back to my throat and I smell ammonia. It's not from any attempt to sanitize the restroom.

We walk out and into the lounge area. Dark figures lay on couches and smoke cigarettes. Chubby girls with make-up jobs you could die from share life stories. Some guy with a hairy chest, who is not pulling off his intended Vampire Lestat look, leans against the wall, staring deeply into the abyss of carbon monoxide. A crowd of people leave a booth in the corner, so we sit down there.

Geber is nowhere around.

"I feel like shit," Meme says.

I take a drag off my cigarette and nod. Meme buries her cigarette butt in the ashtray. One of Meme's junky friends, Grace, notices Meme and flirts a hand and a smile. He looks as if he is about to approach us, but somebody distracts him and he seems to have completely forgotten about her as he sits back down in his booth to drink his water and daydream again. Meme gets up and walks over to his table.

"Frank," Amber says, "how's life at home with the Drama Queen?"

"I thought you guys broke up," Paul says.

"We did," I shrug, "but Meme has a talent for terrorism. I'm a hostage in my own apartment."

"Oh," Amber says, "she's not that bad."

"Yes she is," Paul and I say in unison. Then I say to Amber, "Why don't you try living with her for a day?"

Amber and Paul laugh. I lean over the table.

"She didn't get *the part*," I say.

"That sucks," Amber says. "It's all she ever talked about."

"What's she going to do?" Paul asks.

"Can you imagine Meme with a job?" I ask.

Amber blushes at the thought of it. Paul laughs, digs his fingers in his jet black hair, shakes his head no.

"Meme's fall from grace," Amber sighs, then becomes sympathetic. "Poor thing."

We look over at Meme. She's standing there with a cigarette in her hand, listening to Grace ramble about something. She leans forward with her head slightly turned and strokes the fur collar near her ear, as if trying to follow what he's saying. She finally gives up and walks back toward our table. Grace kind of jerks and this startles a few people near his corner. A couple of strangers wearing black leather walk over to him and after they exchange a few words they laugh. The place becomes filled with their laughter and its echo lasts too long.

"This speed is bunk," Meme says, sitting down in the booth next to me.

I tear a napkin into tiny white specks and drop them into little drops of water and watch them expand. A drag queen struts up and down the aisle and a crowd of cross-dressers cheer. A gold scarf glitters around her neck, tight white pants on a perfect set of thin legs, high white heels, and a red bra over her breasts. A huge blond wig bounces on her head. Her long fake eyelashes flutter below blue mascara.

Paul leans his head against the greasy wall behind the booth, next to a bright pink flyer advertising the services of a therapist:

> Is Your Life Not Turning Out The Way You Want It To?
> Is Your Family Holding You Down?
> Is The World Oppressing You?
> Do You Want To Develop The Tools To Overcome The Obstacles That Victimize You?
> Do You Want To Discover Your Hidden Potential?
> If You Experience Family Problems, Suicidal Tendencies, And Drug Abuse,
> Call
> Carol Porter
> At 679-HELP
> Let Me Help You Make All Of Your Dreams Come True.

Amber points her finger at Paul's head.

"Hand me that," Amber says. "That flyer above your head."

Paul yanks the pink sheet off the wall and reads it. He smirks and nods the cigarette with his lips, then hands the flyer to Amber.

"This is ridiculous," she says.

Meme leans over the table and reads the flyer, then jerks it out of Amber's hands.

"Why don't you just go see a palm reader?" Paul asks. "Have someone read some tea leaves. I'm sure the level of insight is the same." He inhales his cigarette. "Is it just me, or is this era in excess of professed miracle workers cheating the vulnerable and the blind?"

"Things have always been this way," Amber says. "Human beings can't survive without the comfort of their delusions. This just works according to the Law of Supply and Demand. We've reached a heretofore unknown intensity of desperation. So, we're ready to believe anything. Especially if we see it on the television or in a tabloid, straight out of the mouth of someone as ignorant as ourselves. Critical thinking is a hard thing to sell because it doesn't operate with a remote control."

Meme delicately pets the sleeve of her fur coat and lifts her eyes from the ad.

"I'm going to call and make an appointment," Meme says, "first thing tomorrow."

Chapter 4

THEORY OF EVERYTHING

This morning I called to let Cassandra know that I have a little present for her. I told her I have in my possession some of the finest, purest, uncut heroin her sad little eyes will ever see, if she can just make it here for one last appointment. I got some methadone from a clinic this morning because I knew she would want her fix first thing. I was taking my chances. She could walk in, call my bluff, and bail.

I called Mr. Howard and told him I found what he was looking for. She's a little on the wild side, but she's all I have left. I'm sure we can work on her, I said desperately, please meet me at eleven. I broke the golden rule for a saleswoman: Don't ever let your buyer know how desperate you are to sell.

Then a girl named Meme called to make an appointment. She said she found my number on a flyer. I told her to be here at eleven sharp or forget about it. I almost said, spare me your petty problems. Get over whatever. Move on.

At 10:45 Mr. Howard arrives with the buzz of Pinhead's camera. Stump drags his light equipment to my desk and Pinhead leans the ladder against the wall. No point in setting up the equipment until a client shows.

"I'm so glad you could make it," I say.

Mr. Howard sits silently behind my desk. He plugs his mouth with a cigar, flicks the gold lighter, and inhales the flame. He puffs white clouds and lifts his gold Rolex into the smoke that shields his expression. Pinhead leans back on the yellow vinyl couch, stretching his legs across the floor, focusing the camera with his wire-thin fingers. Stump's body is sprawled out on a single cushion.

"She should be here soon," I say.

Mr. Howard raises his eyebrows. He holds the cigar between his lips and bolts smoke out of the corners of his mouth. There is a knock at the door.

I trip over my legs when I turn around. The door opens before I reach the knob. Cassandra's face is full of blisters and red finger scratches, her skin yellow around the eyes. She wears a worn-out black leather jacket and tight leopard pants. Cassandra walks into the room, paces back toward me, her brown Nikes squeaking on the floor.

"Cassandra," I say, "this is Mr. Howard! He's making a TV show!"

"Where is it?" Cassandra asks, wiping the black leather sleeve over her nose. "Carol, where is it?"

I glance over at Mr. Howard; his black mustache limps downward with his frown.

"She needs her medication," I say, handing her the little brown paper sack. "We have a deal, okay?"

Cassandra's fingers tear through the sack. She turns her back on all of us while she checks it out. She scratches her leopard pants and says, "Fucking rash."

"Cassandra," I say, "I want you to talk to Mr. Howard. Sit over here in front of the desk, okay?"

"This ain't dope," she says.

Cassandra springs her skeleton-thin legs and bangs her head into the door, pulls at the knob, and slams the door open against the wall. I rush toward her and try to hold her back, but my hand slides down the black leather sleeve and she's out the door with thirty dollars of synthetic dope.

I run after her down the hallway and out to the corridor. I jump and skip steps down the stairs, look down over the railing, and hear the boom of the front door opening and slamming.

Outside, there is no sign of her.

I scrunch my face to hold back tears and mope slowly up the stairs to my floor. I don't know how I can face Mr. Howard after an episode like this. All hopes are dead at this point. I should have known that it wouldn't work. Cassandra's a hopeless case. But my other two clients weren't even worth calling. It was a last-ditch effort. It was a stupid idea.

From the doorway I see Pinhead with the ladder in his arms, his camera turned off. Stump's tiny mouth frowns, looks regretful to me. I finally look up at

Mr. Howard. His curlicued mustache raises above his cheekbones, his face reddens. The leather briefcase falls from his hand to the floor. He slowly removes the smoky cigar from his mustachioed smile, opens his arms wide, and stutters.

"She's…she's," Mr. Howard's mouth twitches, "she's absolutely perfect!"

I glance at Pinhead, at Stump, back at Mr. Howard.

"She…is?"

"Yes!" he whispers, his other hand over his lips. "She's spectacular!"

But she's gone.

Mr. Howard swings his large black cummerbund-wrapped belly toward me, arms outstretched, and passes by. I turn around and think, he'll never find her.

In the doorway stands a girl dressed in a long white evening gown, fire-red lipstick, a thickly-powdered white face, and black sunken eyes in decadent 1920s fashion.

Mr. Howard holds the cigar with his teeth and claps his fat round palms together.

"Let the show begin!" he says through his cigar.

He flips his hand toward Pinhead and Stump, a signal to set the lights, roll the camera.

A dream maybe. The wrong address. She's looking for a studio audition somewhere. This can't be the girl who called me earlier. The one I almost advised to go to hell. To leave me alone. To show or don't show, I don't care.

"Excuse *moi*," the girl says, flapping her hand to fan herself. "Is this Carol's office?"

"I'm Carol," I say, extending both my hands to shake hers. "Please, come in, oh god, where did you come from?"

"I called you earlier," the girl says. "My name is Meme Lamb."

Mr. Howard circles the girl and shifts the pink feathered boa hanging around her neck so that it hangs symmetrically down her front.

"And this is Mr. Howard," I say.

Mr. Howard turns red, and breathlessly stares into the girl's eyes.

"It is the highest honor to make your acquaintance," Mr. Howard says.

Mr. Howard's fat hand nervously touches a curl of Meme's hair. She slaps his hand away.

"Do you mind if I smoke?" Meme asks.

She attaches a cigarette to a long ivory cigarette holder and lets it hang from her bright red lips. Mr. Howard flicks his gold lighter and lights her cigarette.

"Make yourself comfortable," Mr. Howard says. "Please, sit right here. Is there anything I can get you? Anything?"

"Are these guys going to film me?" Meme asks.

She puffs a stream of smoke toward Pinhead and Stump, gracefully flowing toward the chair with her arms held away from her body. She sits down and crosses one leg over the other, leaning to one side of the chair. She sucks on the ivory cigarette holder, then holds it away from her body to make room for the path of smoke rings directed at Mr. Howard.

"I am producing a live documentary of significant scientific and historic relevance," Mr. Howard says. "A testimony to Carol's groundbreaking contribution to the field of therapeutics and profound ministering to the human condition."

Meme searches her purse and pulls out a mirror to touch up the powder on her face. Mr. Howard stands on the other side of the desk and gestures his arms out in an attempt to embrace her from a distance.

"I hardly know you and I already fancy you as an ideal candidate for this project," Mr. Howard says. "No doubt your talents far exceed the scope of this psychological investigation! You have charisma! Stage presence! A natural draw for attention! This would only be the beginning of the realization of your untapped potential. Your foot in the door, so to speak. All you have to do is let me document your healing process from beginning to end. From a mentally disturbed, angst-ridden young girl to an accomplished, successful lady of achievement."

Meme's eyes signal a warning with a squinted glare. She raises her black painted eyebrows and takes a couple of frustrated drags off her cigarette holder.

"Let's not kid ourselves, okay?" Mr. Howard says, brushing off her smirk with a wink of the eye. "You have come to meet Carol for a therapy session. A wise move if I don't say so myself—for she is a woman of wonders and dedicated one thousand percent to the successful development of her clients. Carol is your ticket to a sound mind! Or everlasting fame and fortune, if you like! Anything your heart desires! I'm only here as a witness. To manufacture evidence to substantiate what I already know: that Carol's eclectic therapy techniques are a sophisticated technological phenomenon in which lies a subtle theory of everything and cure-all for human problems, diseases, and anomalies. All I'm really asking for is your cooperation."

I step toward Meme and scoop her flicked ash out of the air with both hands cupped together.

"I'll even offer the therapy sessions for free," I say, disposing the ash in the trash can to the side of my desk, "to show that your interests are at heart."

I have never been this excited about a client, and I haven't even heard her sob story yet.

Meme straightens and flattens the fabric of the white evening gown.

"You see this button?" Mr. Howard asks, putting a large finger to the side of Pinhead's camera. "All I have to do is push this special red button and we go live throughout the nation. Reality TV! 24 hours a day! 7 days a week! Instant fame!"

"Instant fame?" she asks.

"That's right!" Mr. Howard says. "You give me your consent, and you'll be a star by the end of the week. We'll need a few days to set the stage."

Meme checks her face in the mirror again, presses a finger along the edge of her red lips to sharpen the line of lipstick at the corner of her mouth. She closes the compact mirror and looks up at Mr. Howard, who has his arms outstretched, waiting for a sign from Meme to begin creation. Meme taps the ivory and ashes on my floor.

"A star?" she asks dubiously. "I'll be on TV?"

Mr. Howard bobs his head like a fishing pole.

"Are you ready to take the leap, Meme?" he asks. "To step into an illustrious career of international stardom? To become a celebrity? Rich and famous?"

"Yes," she says. "I think I'm ready!"

Mr. Howard's big round hands clap and clutch together, and he releases a deep breath that sounds like the word, "Yes!"

I sit behind my desk and watch Mr. Howard direct Pinhead to stand at an angle to fit Meme and me in a single frame in order to capture the dynamics of the client-therapist relationship. Mr. Howard asks Meme to inch her chair closer to my desk.

"Good!" Mr. Howard says. "Very good."

Mr. Howard rubs his palms and pinches his lips together, then helps set the ladder and light equipment for Stump. I've almost forgotten what to do, what my objectives are. I'm so amazed that the deal is still on.

Never let someone know how eager you are to buy.

I'll be renegotiating this deal by the end of the day.

"Lights!" Mr. Howard says.

Stump illuminates Meme's face.

"Camera!"

Pinhead's lens buzzes.

"Action!"

Pinhead zooms the camera lens for a close-up of my face.

"So…" I pause, seeking direction from Mr. Howard. He swings an invisible lasso with his hand, a motion for me to continue. "Problems?"

There is a long silence as Pinhead swivels his body in Meme's direction. She waits until the camera is squared adjacent to her face.

"That's an understatement," Meme exhales.

"How is your relationship with your parents?" I ask.

Meme winds her hair around a couple of fingers, then places her hand in front of her mouth and thoughtfully pats her red lips.

"We don't see eye to eye," she says.

"That must be very difficult," I say.

"Yes," she says, twisting her head toward Pinhead's camera, trembling her lips open. "They don't understand the magnitude of my ingenuity. They have no idea."

Meme blows a thick ring of smoke. Mr. Howard shifts the silver shelled light. Stump holds it still.

"Dysfunctional family," I say. "Sorry to hear that."

"Yes," Meme says. "Try living with them."

"That must be traumatic."

"Traumatic," Meme sighs. "Oppressive. And deadly to my individuality and overall purpose in life."

Meme rotates her head away from Pinhead's lens.

"Meme, let's talk about *you*," I say, leaning forward. I delicately tap my temple. "Let's talk about you and your feelings. Tell me what is bothering you."

Mr. Howard quietly rubs his palms together. Pinhead zooms the camera in for a close-up. Meme expresses a noiseless cry.

"Things are *not* turning out the way they are supposed to," Meme says.

She inhales her cigarette.

"What's not turning out right?" I ask, pretending to note something on a notepad on my desk. "What is your family holding you back from?"

Meme's red mouth sulks into a delicate oval shape.

"The things I want," she says.

"What do you want?"

"I want to act," Meme says, spreading her arms out with the pink feathered boa spun around them. "I want to sing."

Mr. Howard kisses the tips of his fingers and says without a sound, "Beautiful!"

"Are you doing these things?" I ask, writing a couple of dollar signs on the notepad, a concerned expression on my face.

Meme bows her head, turns at a slight angle toward the camera, her red lips swell and pout. Stump dims the spotlight. Meme bats her eyelashes, works her lips into a quiver.

"Yes," Meme says. "Well, I'm trying to figure out a way. That's why I'm here. I've been thinking about it a lot, you know, maybe moving to Hollywood. Or maybe Broadway or something."

Mr. Howard slips Meme a white tissue.

"So when are you thinking of doing that?" I ask. "The Hollywood bit. Becoming a star and all that?"

Meme's head tilts down and she looks like she is off in a day dream. Vacant pale blue eyes. Frozen white painted face. One arm hangs tiredly over the arm chair. The long ash at the end of her cigarette limps downward, detaches, and falls to the floor. She slowly lifts her head and looks at me. Her worn face begins to show through the white powder under her eyes.

"I tried out for the leading role...*the part*," Meme says, closing her eyes, quivering her lips against her fingertips as they pinch the ivory cigarette holder. "I didn't get...*the part!*"

Meme's long choppy sigh is filmed at close range by Pinhead's camera. He hovers around her like a sympathetic robot, bobbing his head and panning for various angles. Meme twists her fists into the red hair on her head. Mr. Howard motions for Pinhead to pan a half circle while Meme's face is cupped in her palms.

"You can always try out for another part," I say. "Take some acting classes, dedicate yourself."

The white tissue falls from her grip to the floor.

"Cut!" Mr. Howard says. Pinhead hits a switch on the camera. "That was sublime! Pinhead, I want that falling tissue in slow motion." He hands Meme another tissue. "Meme, that was almost perfect. This time cock your head back with the release, then look down into the eye of the camera when the tissue falls away from your face. Pinhead, try to get her facial expression in the background. Stump, I want that tissue illuminated like the wings of an angel!"

Meme rehearses a few pretentious expressions of horror and practices several Kleenex projections which fall short and rest on the lap of her white evening gown.

Mr. Howard claps his hands.

"Action!"

"Everything is going to be okay," I say. "Meme, everything is going to be okay."

Meme lets go of the Kleenex. She cocks her head back too abruptly and the tissue catches on a red curl of hair. She nods her head, shakes the tissue loose and into the air. Pinhead squats his long legs and follows the tissue as it sways down to the floor. Stump's spotlight is so bright the Kleenex glows with an eerie radiance reminiscent of the kind of light found only in religious pictures. Pinhead glides the camera toward Meme's red head. The back of Meme's hand rests on her forehead, an improvisation that is agreeable to Mr. Howard, who kisses his fist with a red face, his black mustache erect and lively. He motions for me to move on.

"So, you want to be a diva, too?" I ask.

Meme's red head nods while she opens up the cosmetic case again and powders a couple of premature wrinkles.

"Let me get this straight." I'm doodling smiley faces on my note-pad. "Part of you wants to be a singer and part of you wants to be an actress?"

"Yes," Meme says.

She closes the cosmetic case and relaxes in the chair, her posture less confident now than in her debut at my door less than thirty minutes ago. She attaches a new cigarette to her cigarette holder.

"I can help you make these things possible," I say. "Your failures are symptomatic of a special ailment with which I'm especially familiar."

Meme turns her head to her side. Her eyes almost water, but don't. My office is mostly silent but for the hum of Pinhead's camera. Mr. Howard's forearms form perpendicular lines, one across his wide cummerbund and the other straight up his chest to where his fingers stroke the hair on one side of his black mustache.

Mr. Howard waves his hand for Pinhead to back off, and then silently instructs him to stand behind Meme. He points his finger at the bookshelf, at the row of self-help books. A gesture I read as *let's get to the heart of the matter, the marrow of your philanthropic endeavors.*

Stump blasts my eyes with the spotlight. Pinhead, nearly straddling Meme's back, adjusts the focus of the camera. I check the top drawer in my desk for my glasses, pull them out of the case, and push them up along the bridge of my nose. I stand to the side of my certificate.

Meme lifts a hand up to her face, wipes some hair out of her eyes, inhales from the cigarette between two flared fingers.

"I wrote this book," I tell Pinhead's camera, "*The Pigs' Hammer.*" I pull the book from the shelf and display it to the camera, holding it at breast level, off to the side. "I offer a variety of eclectic services, ranging from family therapy to psychotherapy. I have two years of experience in counseling adolescents, adults, children, and couples. I offer treatment for relationships, depression, anxiety and addictions. Mostly, though, I help people like you. People who struggle to achieve their lifelong dreams. People who, for one reason or another, fail to measure up to their full potential. I help my clients overcome the obstacles that have made them so miserable. I help them rebuild the foundations of their life. I do this by helping them confront their issues. Only then can a person become whole. Only then can a person be everything she can be."

Meme's eyes: Tell me I'm beautiful, tell me I'm everything, tell me everything is going to be okay, tell me what I want to hear, make me feel better, tell me the impossible is possible, tell me I'm worth it, tell me life is different. Etcetera.

I skim through the pages of my self-help book to the symptom checklist.

"Meme," I say, "I have to ask you some personal questions. These are very important questions that will help me make an informed and intelligent evaluation of your condition in order to determine a proper method of treatment."

First important question:

"Do you have any memories of your past lives?"

"No," Meme says.

I check the box and note the following: Repressed Memories of Past Lives.

"Do you remember being in your mother's womb?"

"No," she says.

I note the following: Repressed Prenatal Memories.

"Do you ever feel anxiety and stress about your future?"

"Yes," Meme grunts.

Meme has built up tension from not dealing with her issues.

"Do you use drugs and alcohol?"

"I experiment a little."

Drug Addict.

"Were you sexually abused as a child?"

"No."

Incest Victim (in denial).

"Do you sometimes feel that life is meaningless?" I ask.

"Among other things," she says.

Suicidal.

"Do you feel a desire to have control of your life?"

She yawns.

I write down: Desires to take control of her environment to overcome the helplessness she felt growing up in an oppressive and sexually abusive household.

"Do you…"

Pinhead's camera grinds and drones, then fades into silence. The black device rises off Pinhead's miniature head like a helmet, the wires and cords still attached to a pack on his chest.

"I need to change the battery," Pinhead squeaks.

"Everybody take five!" Mr. Howard says.

Pinhead digs through the pack on his chest and pulls out a battery. Stump huffs and puffs while he struggles down the ladder.

"Am I on TV?" Meme asks, starry-eyed. "Are people watching me on TV?"

"Soon they will be," Mr. Howard says. "Millions of people! Throughout the world! Meme, touch up a little under the eyes. Nobody wants to look deeply into the sockets of the soul if they look like pools of muddy water."

She pouts her lips.

"Meme, that's lovely," Mr. Howard says. "Hold that expression. Own it. Make it yours. Believe in it. Stump, where are those refreshments?"

Meme zealously checks her face with the compact mirror again. White powder sprinkles around her face like tiny snowflakes. Stump rattles a tray of tin can sodas around the room and hands out bags of popcorn.

"We need to move along," Mr. Howard says. "What's the next stage?"

"Hypnosis," I say, "then a diagnosis."

"Let's get a move on it," Mr. Howard says.

He puts the cigar in his mouth and walks over to take a look at Pinhead's camera.

I pull a little green bottle of amytal out of my desk. Mr. Howard assists Meme to the yellow vinyl couch and Pinhead and Stump reset the camera equipment.

"Meme," I say, "just let yourself relax. There's nothing to worry about. I'm going to hypnotize you so I can connect with your subconscious self. This is a medication formulated to induce a hypnotic state."

I hand Meme the green medicine bottle. She turns the cap off, tilts her head back, and pours half the bottle into her mouth. Her head remains tilted back, her mouth slightly open, and she squints her powdered eyes. She holds the green bottle to the corner of her mouth like a flask and sips a little more amytal down her hoarse throat. She swallows and coughs, empties the rest of the bottle into her system. Her eyes widen and glisten. The green bottle falls to her lap.

"Action!" Mr. Howard says.

Pinhead swoops toward me for a head shot.

"Meme," I say, "can you hear me?"

I lean over her body to hear her whisper.

"Yes," she says.

"How do you feel right now?" I ask.

"Good," she says.

I caress her hair and soothe the smudged make-up on her cheeks. Meme looks at me through the little crack between her eyelids.

"Your arms are feeling heavy. Your body is becoming lighter and lighter. I'm going to count to ten and when I get to ten you will be sound asleep."

At ten, Meme's eyes close and I tap into her subconscious mind.

"Meme," I say, "you are in a deep trance. Can you hear me?"

"Yes," Meme mumbles.

"You are going way back to when you were a little girl," I say. "I want you to imagine that you are a six-year-old girl lying down in bed and your father is sitting next to you. Is the image in your mind yet? Can you see it? Do you have the image? Do you have the image?"

"Yes," Meme sighs.

"Meme," I say, "is your father touching you? What is your father doing? You are alone with him. Do you have the image? Do you have the image?"

Meme strokes her stomach like it's a thin, frail kitten.

"Yes," Meme whispers, eyes all white and rolled back. "He is with me."

"Meme," I say, "what is your father doing to you? Is he fondling you? What is he doing?"

"I think he's," she flinches, "I don't…know. Touching me."

"Where is he touching you? Your leg? Are you afraid to tell me?"

"He's touching…my hair," Meme breaks down.

"It's okay," I say. "It's okay. Where else? Is he touching you where he shouldn't touch you? Is his hand on your breast? Can you see it? Can you feel it? What is he doing to you now?"

Meme wipes her hand over her mouth, smears a streak of red lipstick across her cheek and down her chin. Removes the powder over the black bags under her eyes.

"Oh no," she gasps, tries to push the air away from in front of her.

"What is he doing now?" I ask. "Is he taking your clothes off?"

Meme's lower jaw draws downward. Her mouth is sickly guppy-faced.

"He's molesting you?" I ask. "Are you naked? What is he doing?"

"Make him stop," she puffs. Meme pants into her palms, then moans, "Ugh!"

"Meme," I say, holding one of her hands tightly, "I'm going to count to three. When I get to three I want you to come out of the trance. Do you understand me?"

"Ugh," she says, pinching her legs.

"One. Two. Three."

Meme opens her eyes and slowly pushes her hands down to cover her crotch. She slurs unintelligible sounds.

"Can you hear me?" I ask. "Meme?"

"Yes," she moans.

Both hands crisscross over her abdomen. I comb her frazzled red hair back with my fingers.

"Meme," I say, "you were molested by your father. You repressed the memories."

Meme mumbles and buckles her body. She slowly places her bony fingers over her face. Mr. Howard glides Pinhead toward the yellow vinyl couch like he's operating the camera by himself.

"Meme," I say, "we need to deal with these issues."

"I don't feel very good," Meme chokes out, smearing more red lipstick over her face.

"I know," I say, placing a hand on her knee and gently caressing her thigh. "You've been through some terrible things. I know how you feel. I have been there. But there is hope." Pinhead pans from left to right. "I guess what I'm saying is," pause, "it's going to take some work."

Mr. Howard hands her a Kleenex. Stump blasts the spotlight

"You must have the courage to heal," I say.

Meme's elegant framework folds on the yellow couch. The white evening gown is wet and wrinkled. She closes her eyes.

"Meme," I say, softly stroking her hollow cheek, "everything will be okay. I can tell just from looking at you that you have what it takes. You are a strong woman. You are a survivor. You can do it. You can be a diva! You can be a star!"

"Cut!" Mr. Howard hollers.

Meme rolls over, her face all swollen and red and black, splotched here and there with white powder and lipstick. She looks like a drunk clown.

Mr. Howard walks with me to the window on the other side of my office. He reaches into his inside pocket and pulls out a fresh cigar, perfuming the air with the sweet scent of tobacco leaf. The smile on his face is undisturbed even with his lips wrapped around the cigar. He lights and puffs, pulls the cigar out of his grin.

"She's as cataclysmic as the Challenger Disaster," Mr. Howard says. "Devastatingly awesome! A woman launched with enough kinetic opportunity to propel her into orbit with the stars and legends, only to shatter into a thousand filaments and remain ground-bound and aimless. Carol, I could kiss you right now." He points his cigar at Meme as she staggers blindly in our direction. "She's a spectacle of advanced political symbolism. A mascot for all those privileged white women who want so desperately to carve themselves a slice of the American pie reserved especially for minorities and the authentically disadvantaged. The dated housewife's protest against domestication and double standards will pale in comparison to the atrocities inflicted upon the modern woman!" He opens his arm toward Meme, bows slightly for a regal introduction. "This here is the greatest victim in the universe!"

Chapter 5

THE CONTRACT

There's a commotion outside. I walk to the window, pull up the blinds, look down the boulevard. A big black Rolls Royce is parked in the middle of the street in front of the apartment building—five cars lined behind it. A fist pumps outside the window of a green Pinto, flips a finger. Other cars honk their horns.

The passenger door opens and a hooker steps out. I see this kind of thing all the time. Limousines, long Cadillacs, relieving prostitutes of their duties. One time, I saw a hooker crawl out of a thirty-footer and four-legged her way to the curb like a car-struck feline.

This whore down below, she stops and lifts her face; it's a face of despair. Meme throws her hands in the air and waves. What's she doing in a Rolls?

I regret not getting out of the house. I wanted to take advantage of the idle time, drink my coffee and smoke my cigarettes in peace. I turned off the ringer, lowered the blinds, thought about what to do with my life and couldn't come up with anything. Let's say I was ruminating.

I light up another cigarette and continue to stare down below. Meme looks pretty beat; I wonder if it's the work of a makeup artist, the latest style. Maybe she passed on the therapist and saw a plastic surgeon. I don't really know. Best not to think about it. I just think to myself, bring it on—let time move forward. I stare up at the sky and wait for a sign.

Meme crashes through the door, or that's what it sounds like. I've learned not to flinch in these situations, not to act epileptic. I have learned not to turn my head.

"Frank, I've heard so much about you!"

The words rumble across the apartment. A surge of adrenaline sends my arms and legs into a paroxysm of horror. I imagine a black beast charging toward me, something the size of a Spanish bull. Before I have time to react, to run for cover, a man of gargantuan proportions—wearing a tuxedo and holding a cigar—grabs my hand and shakes my body like a gored matador. He smiles through a ring of smoke and introduces himself.

"I'm Bill Howard! A pleasure to meet ya!"

Meme looks loaded, swaying beside him, having trouble standing on her feet. She has a large book in one hand and something that looks like a First Aid Kit in the other.

"I'm Frank," I say.

He lets go of my hand.

"I'm a TV producer!" Bill Howard says. "Bill Howard Productions! I've done it all! Talk shows! Soaps! Epic TV specials! Saturday morning cartoons and campaign commercials! And half a dozen films! Though I doubt you've heard of them. Mostly European! Connecticut, actually. I'm looking to do something different! To cover new ground! A brand! New! Approach! Reality TV!"

"A TV producer?" I ask, turning to Meme. "I thought you went to therapy?"

"It was more than a therapy session!" Bill Howard answers. "It was like watching Jesus Christ walk on water! I wish you could have been there! Tell me Frank, have you ever seen a miracle?" He lights the cigar, then holds it between his fingers. "In the space of an hour, Meme learned more about herself than what most people learn in all their years put together! Literally! You could see Meme transform into a different person! Confident! Poised! Self-assured! A woman with a bright future! Ready to open up and share herself with the world! Her eyes sparkled like stars! I've never seen anything so beautiful!"

The white powder on Meme's face is thick and ghostly. The mascara, bleeding around the eyes, makes her look like a famished raccoon. And the red lipstick smudged around her mouth and down her chin—you might think it was blood from gnawing on self-inflicted wounds. She looks like she's been to an exorcism.

"Of course," Bill Howard says, "the Seven Wonders of the World weren't built in a day. I'll need nine weeks or so! This is Reality TV!"

He walks the length of the apartment, surveying the room. He strokes his mustache and nods his enormous head with approval.

"Filming will begin right away!" Bill Howard says, pulling out a packet of papers. "At an undetermined time the show will go 'Live!' on national television! Where and when is to remain a surprise! This could be the most exciting thing that's ever happened! In your life and on television! *The Greatest Show on Earth*! But, Frank, we need your participation! This is 'Reality' we are talking about! You are her boyfriend! You might even be her future husband! Not to get your hopes up." He winks, then puffs the cigar. "I need to show all aspects of Meme's life! What she looks like in the morning! How she eats her food! What she does during her spare time! What she's like when she's alone or just hanging out with you! The whole person! Frank! The whole person! What it's like to be a woman in this modern age! The dreams! The hopes! The desires! The heartbreak! The will to overcome the obstacles of life!"

He hands me a form: the Release and Agreement. I sit down and read:

> By signing below, I hereby consent to the filming and recording of my image and my likeness, for use and reuse by Producer (Bill Howard), and any of Producer's (Bill Howard's) respective licensees, assignees, subsidiaries, parents, or affiliated entities and each of their respective employees, agents, officers and directors (collectively) of my voice, actions, name, appearance, likeness, biographical material, and any information about me (whether true or false), for the use of the Series (entitled "The Greatest Show on Earth"), including, without limitation, any recordings, still pictures, film and video footage, as edited, altered, or modified by Producer (Bill Howard), in any or all media now known or hereafter devised, worldwide in perpetuity, on or in connection with the Series ("The Greatest Show on Earth"), including, without limitation, in advertisements, promotions, publicity, marketing, merchandising, or in any other manner. I agree that the Producer (Bill Howard) may use all or any part of my image and likeness, and may alter or modify it regardless of whether or not I am recognizable. I release the Producer (Bill Howard) from any and all liability arising out of the recording or use of my life, my image, and my likeness. I agree not to make any claim against the Producer (Bill Howard) as the result of the recording or use of my life, my image, and my likeness, including, without limitation, any claim that such use invades my right to privacy or defames me.
>
> By signing this form, to the maximum extent permitted by law, I hereby release Producer (Bill Howard), any television station or channel, cable network, or satellite network that airs the Series ("The Greatest Show on Earth"), the other participants in the Series ("The Greatest Show on Earth"), the advertisers connected with the Series ("The Greatest Show on Earth"), each of their respective parent, subsidiary and affiliated companies, all other persons and entities connected with the Series ("The Greatest Show on Earth"), and

each of their respective officers, directors, agents, representatives, employees, successors, assignees, and licensees from any and all claims, actions, damages, liabilities, losses, costs and expenses of any kind (including, without limitation, attorney's fees) arising out of, resulting from, or by reason of, my participation in the Series ("The Greatest Show on Earth"), including, without limitation, any and all claims, actions, damages, liabilities, losses, costs and expenses of any kind resulting from the actions of another participant or any other third party at any time.

"I know what you are thinking!" Bill Howard says. "'What is so exciting about two people sitting around doing nothing?' This is a return to the basics! The fundamentals of existence! Who needs another *Apocalypse Now* when you can find the chaos of Vietnam inside the bedroom? When there's a war to be fought in the jungle of ourselves? Not to mention it's much more cost-effective. Which doesn't, in my opinion, diminish its virtues! To find splendor in what is normal! The simple pleasures of two young lovers finding their way in the world! You don't have to do anything but go about your daily routine! Your daily rituals! Meme will go to therapy and deal with her issues, and then come home where you can relish the fruits of her labors! A new and improved version of herself!"

"Everything we do will be on television?" I ask.

"With discrimination," Bill Howard says. "I promise, no cameras in the bathroom. What do you say?"

Meme looks so sad and desperate, I shake my head and sign my name. To be honest, I'm even a little giddy about the opportunity. Happily scared. I give Bill Howard the Release and Agreement with my signature at the very end.

"Thank you, Frank!" he says, handing me a carbon-copy of the form. "It will be a good time! One you'll certainly remember! I'll introduce a few props to get the ball rolling! The tendency of Reality will take care of the rest! All I ask is that you be yourselves!" He pauses to look over the apartment one last time. "This studio is great! I won't have to change a thing!"

He turns and walks out the door. Soon after, several men wearing overhauls walk in carrying tool boxes. They screw in new light bulbs, inspect the furniture, tinker with the floors. Then they take a gun-shaped device and punch tiny holes into the ceiling and the walls. I don't see the microphones or the cameras, but I can feel and hear them buzzing in my head. The men move meticulously throughout the apartment, room to room, covering every nook and corner. They soon file out of the studio, closing the door.

Meme and I are left standing there, staring blankly at each other. She limps to the chair and sits down. Her body is stiff and slow. I'm thinking, I would rather watch paint dry than a show about our lives. That's when Meme says:

"I have something to tell you. I was molested by my father."

The sunlight rims an outline of Meme's hair. Her eyes—glossy, waxed, unconscious—glow in the dimly lit room. And I get the feeling that I've seen this shot before. There's no question about it—some third-rate horror film.

Meme opens her purse and pulls out an orange pill container. She pours fluorescent pills into her palm and snatches a pink capsule with her lizard-like tongue.

"What are you taking?"

"Didn't you hear what I said? I was molested by my father."

"Okay, Meme," I say. "You are drugged up. But try to come back to me, just for a moment. This isn't funny."

"My father raped me," she says.

"It's been a busy day," I play along. "A therapy session, an audition for television, a little child molestation. What else did you do? Fly to the moon?"

Meme closes her eyes.

"You don't believe me," she says.

She places the back of her hand on her forehead.

"Okay," I say awkwardly. "When did this happen?"

She blinks her mascara-caked eyelashes.

"I don't know," she says.

"You don't know?" I ask.

Meme pinches the bridge between her eyes with her fingers.

"I don't remember...yet," she says.

"You don't *remember*?" I ask.

"I don't have all the memories...yet," she says.

"You were molested by your father, but you don't *remember* being molested by your father?"

"Yes," she says. "The memories are repressed."

How can you know what you don't know?

I walk over to the coffee table and look at the red, white and blue case, which is conveniently labeled: Sex Victim Kit. Right next to it is *The Pigs' Hammer: Preying on Sexual Predators*. Below the title, reads: *A Book for Victims of Sex Abuse*. I look through the Sex Victim Kit and find a large brown sack of pill containers. I read some of the labels. Halcion. Xanax. Ativan. Prozac. I find a large white diaper that crackles in my hands. A rubber nipple. A candy cane. I find *The Pigs' Hammer Workbook* and a box of crayons. A movie cassette with *Sybil* printed on the label. A stamped envelope with FATHER written on it, address to be filled in. At the bottom of the box is a necklace with a yellow Star of David.

"Meme," I say, "what did you get us into?"

After Meme takes a shower and scrubs the layers of powder and lipstick off her face, she lays herself out on the couch, cuddling a little blue blanket. I clear off the coffee table and set up the television and VCR. Meme came up with the idea for us to watch the movie *Sybil* so I can understand her newfound disease. She reaches her hand into the light brown crumpled sack and eats a pill like it's a puffed kernel of popcorn.

An unattractive nerd named Sybil is molested and gets an enema up the butt. Her tongue hangs out of her mouth and she screams behind huge, god-awful eyeglasses that hide her face. She changes her name dozens of times. She takes on different personalities and perfects the art of role-playing. She forgets who and what she is and loses time. She breaks glass windows and runs around bent over like the Hunchback of Notre Dame. Dr. Wilbur, the therapist on hand, stupendously attempts to rationalize the irrational. Tries to put a puzzle back together out of the pieces she helped fragment from Sybil's character.

As far as film reviews go, I give it two thumbs up in the surreal department. There's a cool scene where Sybil growls like a dog. Even Meme laughed at that.

I push the rewind button on the VCR.

"I'm not sure I understand," I say, though I'm afraid I understand all too clearly.

Meme digs something out of the Sex Victim Kit. Another pill—bright yellow.

"The abuse I endured growing up with my family was so traumatic I repressed it," Meme says, now somewhat perky, "and if I want to get better, I need to confront my issues, just like Sybil. I have to work on my memories before I can be whole again."

"But how can you know that you were molested if you don't remember being molested? What if you are mistaken?"

Meme picks up *The Pigs' Hammer* from the end table. She hands me the book.

"I have a lot of symptoms," Meme says. "If you want to understand me, then you should study this book. We can read it together every night before we go to bed."

"Every night?" I ask. "Together?"

"Yeah," Meme says. "We can read it in the morning too!"

I nod, slowly.

I open *The Pigs' Hammer* and turn to the page of contents and read the titles of each chapter. The first section is called "Why You Are Depressed." The second section is called "Secrets of Success." The third section: "The Inner Child." The fourth: "For Supporters of Victims." The fifth section is called "Courageous Womyn Tell All." The appendix is called "The Checklist."

I can feel the wrinkles roll together on my forehead—a throbbing headache.

"This is convenient," I say.

Meme turns the pages for me.

"Here," she says, pointing at the title of the last section of the book. "This is the symptom checklist. Read it. You'll see. Everything makes sense."

I look at the chapter heading: "The Checklist." I scan the pages and read:

> The following are some of the symptoms of incest. If you or anyone you know has any of the following characteristics, then more than likely you are a victim of child abuse. If you answer yes to any of the following questions, you can be certain that you are a sex victim. If you have fuzzy memories of abuse, or no memories at all, it is more than likely you were abused.
>
> Do you feel sad sometimes?
> Do you feel cheated in life?
> Do you have eating disorders?
> Are you a slacker?
> Do you ever feel stressed out?
> Were you in daycare?
> Are you humorless?
> Are you funny? (Do you use humor to disguise how *bad* you feel inside?)
> Are you a risk taker?
> Are you afraid to take risks?
> Do you watch too much TV?
> Do you ever feel guilt?
> Have you experienced a pattern of being a victim?
> Are you an underachiever?
> Do you have marital problems?
> Are you a procrastinator?
> Are you impulsive?
> Are you a sensation seeker?
> Are you easily bored?
> Are you easily distracted?
> Do you have gastrointestinal problems?
> Do you ever get headaches?
> Do you have arthritis?

Do you have cancer?
Do you have AIDS?
Do you lack discipline?
Are you worrisome?
Are you insecure?
Do you have financial difficulties?
Do you have mood swings?
Do you feel different and left out?
Do you have regrets?
Do you drink alcohol?
Are you disillusioned?

I look up from the book.

"This can't be serious," I say. "It's a joke, right? Just part of the show?"

"Frank," Meme says, "this isn't a joke."

We both sit there silently for what seems like an entire minute. And I keep thinking, this is a joke. It has to be. Meme is playing around with me. This is Mr. Howard's morbid fantasy. Or is it? I'm getting confused. Is she acting or is this for real? You would think there would be some kind of prevention program to see that things like this don't happen. Some kind of pesticide to protect the whole human crop from such quackery. This can't be for real.

Meme is known for blowing everything out of proportion. Maybe her father accidentally bumped against her or walked in on her in the bathroom and she's taking it all the wrong way. Maybe the therapist picked up the ball and ran too far with it. Maybe this is everything Bill Howard ever wanted.

I don't know whether to be an ass or a sentimental fool. Just be yourself. I decide to play it cool. I don't know what else to do.

"So what now?"

Midnight. I'm sitting on the bed with Meme. She is wearing a small pink dress that would fit a ten-year-old perfectly. The waistband is slightly below her breasts. The dress hangs down to her hips and is more revealing than a miniskirt.

The only thing I want right now is a good night's sleep.

"Now...do it," Meme says, wagging her red pigtails, a candy cane outstretched in her hand.

"Meme," I say tiredly. "I don't think this will..."

"Please?" she pleads, pouring some pills from an unidentified orange pill container into her mouth.

She cups my right hand in both of her hands, raises it to her lips and taps little kisses all over my fingers.

"No," I say wearily.

"Please?" she asks, "just do it."

"Don't you think this is a little strange?" I ask, looking around the room.

"Come *on*," she says.

"Why?" I ask.

"I need to recover all my memories and personalities so I can integrate them and be whole again," Meme says.

"I need for you to leave me alone so I can go to sleep," I say. "It's late."

Meme sits up straight. The bottom of the pink dress rides up above her hips. She is wearing Mickey Mouse underwear.

"Just take the candy cane, here," she says, forcing the candy cane into my hand.

"I'd prefer not to," I say.

"Come on," she insists, holding her palm open.

"Now what?" I ask. "You want me to eat this?"

I take the clear wrapping off the candy cane. If I eat it, the game will be over.

"That's for me," she says. "Tell me you have some candy for me."

I look at Meme. Her red pigtails, the pink ribbons, the glossy eyes.

Meme says, "Say something like, 'Hey little girl, do you want some candy?' and, you know…fondle me."

"I'd prefer not to," I say.

"Do you want me to get better?" Meme asks.

I try to give the candy cane back to her but she refuses to take it.

"Yes," I say, "that's why I'm not going to do this. Now you are one step closer to becoming normal."

"I can't believe you," she says.

She trembles and grabs a pill container from the nightstand. She calms down all of the sudden, and turns toward me.

"Do you want me to get better?" she asks, in a little girl's voice.

A different personality already?

"Oh, Meme," I say.

"I'm not Meme," Meme says. "My name is Sue."

"Alright, Sue," I say, giving up.

What the hell. I want to get some sleep tonight. I can only take so much.

"Okay, say it," she says.

"Sue…" I pause.

"SAY…IT!" she screams.

"Uhh, hey…little…girl…" I stop.

"FRANK...PLEASE?" she begs.

"Do you want some candy?" I ask.

"Yes," she says, in baby-talk.

"Okay, here," I say.

I drop the candy cane on her lap and grab a blanket from the bed. I could sleep in the bathroom, but the lock is broken. I could sleep on the streets—it would be safer. I hear an instant, ear-drum-infecting scream come from behind me while I walk toward the door.

"GET...BACK...HERE!" Meme says.

"What do you want?" I turn around. "I gave you the candy cane and that's what you wanted and I said, 'Hey little girl...'"

She shakes her head.

"*What*? What can I do? What do you want?" I ask. "Why are we doing this?"

"We are doing this to help me remember and now you have to touch me," Meme says. "You have to molest me."

I turn away from the stoned look in her eyes.

"Meme, this is sick," I say. "This isn't therapy. This is a voluntary lobotomy. This is a New Age voodoo experiment and you are the unlucky subject. You have to see that. Don't you? Please tell me you see that..."

"Frank, I'm trying to remember the Candy Man," Meme pouts. "Everybody in the group has a Candy Man."

"What group?"

"The Support Group," she says. "The Women's Support Group. And I want to be ready for my first session."

"But what if you *don't* have a Candy Man?"

"But I do," Meme says.

"How do you know," I ask, "since you need so much help to remember?"

"I can tell...everybody can tell," she says. "It is obvious."

"How is it obvious?" I ask.

Meme throws herself back on the bed and exercises her fists over her eyes like she's grinding away tears, kicking her feet on the mattress. I lay down on the couch and pull the blanket over my head.

She succumbs to reading aloud some incest stories from The Big Sex Abuse Book. I hum loudly to block out her voice. She raises her voice. I hum vociferously. And so on. This exchange continues for about an hour, until my throat is hoarse and silent, and I lay defeated and listening to yet another survivor's morbid account about a childhood enema.

All the stories sound so much alike, it puts me to sleep.

Chapter 6

SWINE

Mr. Howard is dressed in a white tuxedo and holding a large microphone labeled: BILL HOWARD'S REALITY TV. He ordered some extras from a local talent agency to fill the streets. He also tipped off a few local news stations. For some people, he said, this is really happening.

Stump and two other midgets are practicing a juggling routine, stumbling around in oversized black shoes and baggy patched diamond-patterned clothes, walking in circles on the front lawn. Red bulbous rubber noses glow on their white painted faces.

"This is starting to resemble a circus," I caution.

"Where's your spirit?" Mr. Howard says. "It's a beautiful day! I can't just leave Stump out of the action! You wait and see! Stump performed this very same clown-as-juggler routine on the Bill Howard Saturday Morning Kiddy TV Show and received 20,000 illegible fan letters by the end of the week! Five year olds just love this stuff! And that's a market you shouldn't scoff!"

Stump balances an orange ball on his red rubber nose.

"I just don't want to give anybody the wrong impression," I say.

"The last thing you should worry about is your image!" Mr. Howard says, instructing me with his cigar. "There is nothing more noble than protecting children from abuse! You are the personification of a good intention!"

Pinhead positions the camera near the front door. Mr. Howard begins a brief interview that we rehearsed in the car ride over.

"Welcome to Bill Howard's Reality TV!" Mr. Howard says. He holds the microphone to his face with one hand and the cigar to his mouth with his other. He looks into the lens of Pinhead's camera. "Carol Porter has recently arrived at the Lamb's house! Carol, would you please describe the nature of this visit?"

"It is my duty to make an inquiry, to investigate, to discover whether or not Mr. Lamb has molested his other children like he raped and sodomized Meme," I say. "As a CPS worker, I have the right to inspect Mr. and Mrs. Lamb's home and their children. After my investigation, I have the State's authority to determine whether or not their children should remain at home, or be moved to a safer and more secure environment, such as my office."

Mr. Howard signals for Pinhead to capture coverage of the juggling act on the front lawn.

"Carol," Mr. Howard says, "don't stand directly in front of the door. I want to get you and Mr. Lamb in a single frame when he steps outside!"

Black uniformed troopers march around Mr. Lamb's house, hiding behind large navy blue shields and impeccably trimmed green bushes. Clubs swing in steel belt rings. Rifle barrels poke out from ivy leaves.

I now have a dozen CPS workers, recruited by Mr. Howard from a local chapter of Narcotics Anonymous. They all look so professional in their tunics and black CPS armbands you can hardly tell that they are a group of uneducated, deranged, psychotic drug addicts.

The sheriff comes walking out of the crowd and lumbers his large body up the gray slate steps. I notice someone peeking through the curtains in a window.

"It's about time," Mr. Howard tells the sheriff. "Okay! Are we ready?"

I nod and Pinhead waves at Mr. Howard.

"Action!"

A warm sensation tingles through my face. My cheeks blush. Pinhead's camera grinds and five or six big cameras from local news teams immortalize my cause.

This is more than I ever hoped for.

I knock on the door. Mr. Howard tells the sheriff to get away from the front of the camera.

The door opens to a man wearing dark slacks, black shoes, and a white collared shirt with the sleeves rolled up to his elbows. He's wearing thick black frames, staring at me through his bifocals, blinking his eyes each time a camera flashes.

"My name is Carol Porter," I say.

"I'm George Lamb," he says. He glances at Mr. Howard, gives him a warm smile. "Are we going to be on TV today? My wife told me that you called."

He laughs.

"I'm...I'm," I say, looking at Mr. Howard, drawing a blank about the lines we rehearsed. Has this guy been waiting for me? "My name is Carol. I'm...Meme's therapist. You must be Meme's father?"

"Yes," he says. "She's not here right now. I didn't know Meme was in therapy."

Mr. Lamb shakes his head at the flashes of light coming from his lawn. His mouth opens and he turns to a woman who steps beside him in the doorway. Her dark red hair is in a bun, forming three or four tight knots on each side of her head that look like red rose buds. Her slim body is draped elegantly in a dark red dress. She smiles brightly above a string of pearls, says, "Hello, Mr. Howard."

"This is my wife, Ellen," Mr. Lamb says.

"We've been expecting you," she says.

"Hello, my name is Carol Porter," I say. "I'm Meme's therapist. I need to ask you a few questions. Routine questions. May I come in?"

"What are the police doing here?" she asks. "I thought this had something to do with a TV show."

"I'm here to investigate some allegations that your husband has molested his children," I say.

Pinhead zooms over my shoulder. Mr. Howard holds the Reality TV microphone to Mr. Lamb's lips.

"What are you talking about?" Mr. Lamb asks. "I haven't molested my daughters. Where would you get that..."

"I learned from Meme that she was raped and molested..."

"Are you kidding?" Mr. Lamb asks. "Is this some kind of *Candid Camera*? How am I supposed to react to a thing like that?"

"It isn't the kind of thing one makes up," I say.

"There has been some mistake," Mrs. Lamb blushes. "Are we really on TV? Is this part of the show? Because if it is, this isn't very funny."

"I need to see your other children," I say.

I take a step between Mr. and Mrs. Lamb, getting a foot in the doorway. Mr. Lamb pushes my upper arm, not letting me pass.

"You can't do this," Mr. Lamb says. "You can't come into my house."

Applause comes from the crowd on the front lawn. I look over and see a group of people gathered around Stump and his midget friends. They are doing somersaults on the lawn, bumping into each other and falling down.

Mr. Lamb is perspiring on his upper lip. His wife and I exchange glances.

"Mr. Lamb, listen," I say. "You can either allow me to perform this investigation now, at your house, or later, after your children have been taken away from you. I have come to your house, *in good faith*, to follow up on an allegation that your children are being sexually abused. Don't you think it would be suspicious if you were to hinder this investigation? Don't you think that that might look like you are trying to hide something?"

Mr. and Mrs. Lamb look at each other and then step away from the door to let me in. Pinhead follows Mr. Howard, who is holding his microphone in front of Mr. and Mrs. Lamb. They are both speechless.

A family portrait in a gold frame hangs on the living room wall. In the picture, Mr. Lamb is standing between his wife and Meme with his arms around both of them. He is wearing a black suit and Meme and Mrs. Lamb are both wearing white dresses. Then I notice the boy and girl standing in front of them in the picture.

"Are these your other children?" I ask.

"Yes, that's my son and youngest daughter there," Mrs. Lamb says nervously into Mr. Howard's microphone.

Her bony hand, the one with the wedding ring on it, reaches over my shoulder. Her index finger points at the girl.

"That's Jill," Mrs. Lamb says, then moving her finger over to the boy, "and that is our only son, Edward."

She brings her hand to her lips.

I take the picture down off the wall.

"I would like to have a word with her," I say, pointing at the little blonde headed girl in the picture. "Where is she?"

"She's upstairs," Mrs. Lamb says, turning pale.

She walks out of the dining room and I hear her footsteps on the stairs. It is silent in the living room. I tuck the family portrait under my arm.

"I want to speak with a lawyer," Mr. Lamb says.

I hear footsteps and the melody of a boy and girl talking and laughing. I turn just as Mrs. Lamb walks back into the living room with Edward and Jill. An old couple, Meme's grandparents, I suppose, tiptoe their old bones behind Mrs. Lamb. Mrs. Lamb whispers something to the children. Jill is wearing a pink dress with a white frilled collar that comes down in a heart shape at her neck. The pink dress has little white tulip prints.

"My name is Carol," I say, smiling the way one smiles at a child. "You will need to come with me."

Mr. Lamb stares at me, his thick black plastic glasses positioned at the center of his long nose.

"I want you to get out of my house right now," Mr. Lamb says, rushing toward me. "Get away from my children…"

Mr. Howard holds the microphone in front of Mr. Lamb's face.

"Mr. Lamb, do you care to comment on the allegations of abuse?" Mr. Howard asks while fighting him off with the microphone.

Pinhead backpedals down the hall while two police officers enter the house and approach Mr. Lamb.

"You're under arrest."

"Why?" Mr. Lamb asks, his hands up in front of his body. "I haven't done anything."

"You have been convicted," the officer says, "I mean…accused of child molestation."

Mrs. Lamb cries out and bends her head down into her palms. The rose buds in her hair are coming undone.

"But," Mr. Lamb says, shaking his head no, fending off the policemen, "I haven't…I didn't…"

Mr. Lamb wavers at the doorway, open arms, shrugging in disbelief. Reporters wave microphones above the crowd of people like a tribe of headhunters anxiously shaking their spears. Cameras flash, blinding Mr. Lamb.

"I haven't done anything," he says. "I don't know what she is talking about."

"Look at him," someone says. "He is a swine!"

Mr. Lamb bulges and quivers like a werewolf.

"What…what…what is happening to me?" he stutters. "What are you doing to me? Stop this…"

I imagine his white collared shirt shredding around his body, pink lop-ears sprouting from his head like devil's horns and heaving forward over his forehead and dangling in front of his eyes. Then I imagine a broad snout protruding from the center of Mr. Lamb's face, bubbling snot out his nostrils, mangling the eye-glasses on his face.

Mr. Lamb will never look the same again. He can deny it all he wants, but his denials will just come out like a series of squeals. The gibberish of pig Latin.

Mr. Howard positions Pinhead for a close-up.

"He's a swine," someone yells.

"Swine! Swine!"

"Daddy," Jill runs for her father's arms.

I wrap my arms around her waist and pull her back before she reaches him. Jill kicks wildly, twisting in my arms like a large fish. I have to pull on her hair because it's the only thing I can get a strong hold on.

Mr. Lamb froths at the mouth, and just as he brings his hands in to cover his pig-face, cloven hooves stretch out of the ends of each arm and a coat of rust-colored bristles blanket his body. Mr. Lamb's black leather wing-tip shoes split open and hooves tap around on the stone steps while Mr. Lamb struggles to keep his balance. He madly snorts into Mr. Howard's Reality TV microphone. Of course, this isn't really happening. It just looks that way to everybody watching television.

Cameras blink on and off. A loud siren approaches. The police try to close in on him while the mob roars with condemnation.

"Rapist!"

"Baby-killer!"

"Child molester."

The police draw near.

"Kiddy Rapist!"

"SWINE! SWINE! SWINE!"

"Kill the mother-fucker."

"I am not a swine," he snorts.

Mr. Lamb's voice is changing.

Edward clutches his mother's side, digs his face into her hip.

Mr. Lamb looks down at himself, blinking each time a camera flashes.

The police circle him, thumping black batons into their hands. A silver streak of badges trace around Mr. Lamb.

"I am not a child molester," Mr. Lamb cries out from his bloated pig-face. The black glasses barely fit his broad snout. "I am not a swine!"

"You look like a swine," one police officer says.

"Yeah," another cop says. "And you're speaking gibberish."

"He's a swine!"

"Arrest him!" Mr. Howard shouts.

Mr. Lamb snorts and wags his head, whipping his imaginary pink pig ears against his temples. Pinhead looms over Mr. Lamb. A police officer asks him to step back.

"Why do you look like a swine, eh?" a cop asks. "You want to explain that one to me?"

"I don't," he says.

"Maybe you look like a swine," one police officer says, grinding the end of his billy club into Mr. Lamb's potbelly, "because you are a swine."

"You're under arrest," an officer says, handcuffs in hand, reaching for Mr. Lamb's hooves.

"My...rights," Mr. Lamb pushes the officer away. "What about my rights?" Snort. "You have to read me my rights!"

Snort. Snort. Snort.

"You have the right to remain suspiciously silent," the police officer says, clutching a hoof. "Anything you say will make you look guilty and will be used against you in the press."

Mr. Lamb swings his fists, knocking an officer to the ground. A black club bashes into his snub nose and shatters the glass in the black plastic frames on his face. Blood drips over his lips.

"I am nnocentiay ntiluay rovenpay uiltygay," Mr. Lamb says. "Oh God!"

"Shoot him!"

Mr. Lamb bucks up and down and shakes his head while a squad of policemen wrestle him to the ground.

"Oh God!" Mrs. Lamb cries.

An eerie sound comes out of Mr. Lamb's mouth, then an animalistic whine from his nose. Mr. Lamb's attempt to resist arrest is met with a bash into his forehead. One baton swipes across his mouth, shattering several front row teeth. Black batons whip through the air and disappear into the circle of policemen. Mr. Lamb is no longer visible. Only the hollow sounding head blows, more eerie squeals.

"Hang him!"

"Justice for the children!"

Mr. Howard looks disappointed when the police stop bashing Mr. Lamb's body. I hear him arguing with the sheriff.

"We need to do another take," Mr. Howard says. "My cameraman was pushed away from the riot and there wasn't a cleared path to allow for a decent shot of the action. This is supposed to be Reality and my audience couldn't see a thing! I'll be lucky if a single frame is worth keeping for the documentary." Mr. Howard's mustache is drooping. "It could have been a dozen policemen piled on top of a kitten, for all my audience knows!"

But the sheriff won't budge. Mr. Howard will have to do some clever editing. Somebody working with special effects could make an actor look like an alleged child abuser.

Mr. Lamb is mangled on his front lawn, blood pouring out of his mouth. His snout is torn apart, hanging in different directions. Teeth fall from his mouth as he coughs. His cloven hooves are cracked open like squashed snail shells. The police drag his broken body through a swarm of reporters to a black van. In the background, a crowd applauds Stump's juggling act.

People are packing up and leaving, but the show isn't over yet. Mr. Howard is negotiating with a talent agent. He wants the protesters to stay a little while longer.

"In order to make 'Reality' more entertaining," Mr. Howard says.

I turn to Mrs. Lamb and find her shivering in her own sweat, holding Edward against her breast. Mrs. Lamb is moving her head from left to right like a metronome, in perfect rhythm. Jill is either in shock or else she has tired of the struggle. She lays over my arm like a dead soldier.

"Come on, Mrs. Lamb," I say and hold my hand out toward her. I motion my finger for her to walk up to me. "Come on, give me Edward."

Mrs. Lamb continues to shake her head and wipes one hand on her wrinkled red dress. Pinhead positions for a face shot.

"No...no...no...no," Mrs. Lamb says, over and over.

"Come on," I say.

"No...no...no," she says, pressing Edward into her body.

A few police officers help pry them apart. Mrs. Lamb faints, falls right on her back, her eyes still open. Edward is hauled to the black van where his father is handcuffed.

I carry Jill to the front door, down the stone steps, and across the lawn. I pass the hoard of Reality TV extras and arrive at Mr. Howard's limousine.

A photographer asks me if she can take a picture of me holding the girl. Jill hangs over my right arm, drooping like a wilted flower.

"Smile for the camera!" says the photographer.

How can I not smile? This is the moment I've been waiting for my entire life.

Chapter 7

911

Toys clutter my apartment: dolls, stuffed animals, stacks of coloring books. Meme is dressed in her white Armani gown, which she says is the type of gown a priestess wears at a Satanic ceremony when a virgin is slaughtered. A silver pentagram hangs down her front. She holds up a Satanic ritual coloring book to show me her artwork. She has colored a little puppy dog brown with black-red knife wounds all over its body; the dog smiles while standing in a puddle of pink and orange blood.

Meme has been telling me about the time she gave birth to triplets at a Satanic ritual when she was eight years old. Her father, the High Priest, slit their throats and made Meme drink their blood. Then he ate their hearts (which is, according to Carol's self-help book, common for Satanists—practically their favorite dish) and then made Meme nurse the torn up fetuses. This story does not corroborate the stories Meme has told me about her alien offspring. Supposedly, she is the mother of thousands of alien babies wandering around the galaxy. I guess only a few of them were slaughtered and gutted by her father. This also happened when she was just eight years old on some faraway planet known as Zorko. *And*, when she was eight years old, the Pope knocked her up, so the story goes; she has several little runts running around the Vatican. Coincidentally, she remembered these experiences after reading all about them in The Big Sex Abuse Book.

A real tear drips down Meme's cheek as she strokes the wounds on the crayon-colored dog.

"The Satanic Cult slaughtered Ralph in a ritual." Meme closes her eyes and wipes a tear with the back of her hand. "They made me eat Ralph!"

"Ralph was hit by a truck," I remind her, "the day after you auditioned for the part in the movie. Remember? Or is *that* a repressed memory now?"

Meme crumples the coloring book in her hand. She wipes it over the tears on her cheeks like it's a Kleenex. She moans and rips out the colored pages, flinging the sheets of paper into the air.

The phone rings, startling Meme out of her mourning and into a hyper-paranoia.

"What if it's the sex-ring people?" Meme digs her fingernails into my wrist. "What if they are watching us, waiting to steal me?"

"What if it's the casting director," I ask, "wanting to fire you for being the worst actress I've ever seen."

"Do you have any idea what I have been through?"

"No," I say. "And apparently, neither do you."

Meme presses all of her fingers into her cheeks.

"The Satanic Cult is coming after me," Meme grabs at her virginal gown. "They want to kill me. Do you want them to take me away?"

"They already have," I say. "You. Me. Your entire family. You'll see."

Meme hunches over the kitchen table with a cigarette in her mouth, writing a letter to her father. Whenever Meme gets a creative block, she consults The Big Sex Abuse Book for some fresh ideas. She asked me to be at her side while she goes through the tumultuous experience of putting it all down.

So I sit on the other side of the little kitchen table while Meme reads through the book, takes notes, and writes a few sentences in the letter.

"Do you want to read the first draft?" Meme asks, holding up the sheets of paper.

"No," I say. "I've had to listen to it. That was enough."

"But I've added some new things," Meme says, "things I haven't told you."

"And I want to thank you for holding out."

Meme drops her head onto the table. I can see that this is going to go nowhere pleasant. The letter:

> *Daddy,*
>
> *I now know what you did to me. I know why I'm so fucked up. I know why life is so horrible. Why nothing ever works out. You molested me when I was a baby and a child and a teenager. You raped me. I remember*

everything. You need help. You are a child molester. I will never talk to you again. I hope they kill you and rape you in prison; that's where you are going to spend the rest of your life. I remember. Ever since the day I was born you would come into my room and molest me. You brought all your friends over and tied me to the bed and they were lined up down the block. You charged them and made money by selling my body. I remember all the ritualistic abuse when you made me have babies. You sacrificed them and made me drink their blood and eat their flesh. I don't know if I'll ever be able to have a baby again. I know if you are still around you will kill it and make me eat it. I am a survivor. I was exploited. I remember you torturing me when I was three years old. I have all the symptoms. I will remember more during hypnosis in future therapy sessions and I will have to confront you. This is part of the healing process. I plan on confronting all of my abusers. I now have someone who really cares about me, someone who understands all the pain I've been through: Carol. She is a wonderful woman. She is amazing. Carol helped me remember that you and mom and grandpa and grandma and your brothers and sisters gang raped me. I remember now. You made me kill people with knives and you made me bury them in the front yard. You locked me in a cage and penetrated me with machinery. You are not my father anymore. I need to detach from you so I can heal. You made me drink goats' blood. I only need my therapist.

I HATE YOU,

Meme

"What do you think?" Meme asks. "All the things I've been through."

She sighs, trying to be strong through these most difficult times.

"I don't know," I say. "What do I think? I think this is getting old."

"It's from a long time ago," Meme says. "But I think there is more."

She opens the book and flips through the pages to the chapter called "Courageous Womyn Tell All," the chapter where women tell their own personal accounts of incest in pornographic detail.

"I must be strong," she sighs, hovering over the thick-leafed book. She reads quietly for five seconds. "I think this happened to me, too!"

"What?" I ask, trying to sound as eager as she is to learn of the most recent disgusting memory. "What memory do you have now? You were kidnapped by time traveling bandits who took you back to the Roman Empire to be one of Caligula's sex slaves?"

Meme sighs, repositions herself on the chair.

"This passage," she says. "I just read it and it helped me remember that I went through this, too."

"Maybe you should get your memories from a different source," I say. "Try to get a balance of both good and bad ones. Some variety. Some different flavors. Mix a little chocolate with the goat's blood, so to speak."

"You don't want to hear it, do you?" she asks.

"No, I really don't."

I light a cigarette. Meme reads from the book anyway.

"I thought you were going to tell me your newest memory?" I ask.

"I am," Meme says, staring at me, confused.

"But you are reading from a book," I say, pointing at *The Pigs' Hammer*.

Her face says: *Duh!*

"I thought you were going to tell me *your* memories," I say, pushing the threshold of a hostile tantrum.

"This is *my* memory," Meme says, pointing down at the passage in the book.

"But that's," I say, leaning over the book, looking at the title above it, "Starglory Womyn's memory."

"But I have the same memory," Meme sniffles. She pulls the book away from me. "Many women have the same stories because this kind of abuse is very common."

The phone rings and I pick it up to avoid Meme's latest X-rated fabrication. A voice explodes through the receiver.

"Is Meme Lamb there?" a girl asks.

"Who is this?"

"I'm a fan of hers," the girl says. "Please let me talk to her. I want to know everything about her. I want to know every detail. I want to be just like her. Everybody loves her."

"How did you get this number?"

"It was on TV," she says.

"Really?" I ask. "This phone number?"

"Yes," she says.

"What channel?" I ask.

She tells me the channel.

"Please, may I talk to Meme?"

"It's The Cult," I say, handing Meme the phone.

Meme shakes the phone up to her ear.

"Hello," Meme says and chews on her lower lip. There is a timid pause. "Same here!" She relaxes back into her chair, strokes her hair. "I have a personality called Cleopatra! That's so cool!" Pause. "Thank you. It makes me feel good to know that someone cares. You too. Thank you."

Meme says goodbye and hangs up the phone. I look for the remote control. The phone rings again.

"Hello," I say to the phone. "Meme's Hotline."

"Hi," a girl says anxiously, "I just wanted to call and tell Meme that I think she is incredible. Do you think she would, uh, talk to me or something? I just want to hear her voice, that would be so awesome!"

"It's The Cult again."

"Tell whoever it is that I'm busy writing a letter to my father," Meme says. She inhales her cigarette and turns the page in her book.

"I'm sorry," I say, "Meme's busy writing the Tragi-comedy of her life."

When I hang up the phone, it rings again.

"Hello," I say. "You have reached Meme's Hotline. How can I help you?"

"Hello, I'm a Cult victim like Meme and…"

I hang up the phone.

It rings again.

"Meme's Hotline."

Nothing.

"Hello," I say.

There is only a sharp pitched breath snapping here and there through the telephone's electrical current. I ask who is there, and the vibrato of a girl's cry raises to a shriek and cuts off just as quickly. She says something, but I'm not sure if it's what I think she said.

"What'd you say? I can't hear you."

"I'm bleeding."

It sounds like the line is dead. A vapid whimper falls faintly audible through the receiver.

"Who is this?"

I can hear her struggling against her breath.

"April. April Laurels."

"Are you okay?"

"I need to talk to Meme. I need help. My dad is molesting me."

Her voice dies, either covered by her own hands or worse, strangled.

"April? Are you still there? Are you okay? What's going on?"

Meme looks up from her letter, and sighs. Rolling her eyes, she reaches for the phone, yanks it out of my hand, and throws a sheet of paper at my face. It's scrawled with her latest plagiarism. Meme jerks the phone to her head and says, "Hello." Sighing repeatedly into the receiver, she smirks grotesquely, in disbelief.

I look at the letter in my hand. I wonder when I'm going to get one of these.

"That's *nothing* compared to what I've been through," Meme says into the phone. "My dad made me *swallow*!"

The rest of her letter:

> ps: And just a few other things, now that I think of it. I remember when you used to rape me you would tell me that if I told anyone you would cut my tongue into thin strips of proscuitto. That is why I live on the edge. I have to learn how to be a little girl again because you raped my innocence from me. How can I become a great success after what you have done to me? No wonder this past year has been so unproductive. I was your sex slave when I was a child! You are sick! Every morning you woke up smiling and whistling Dixie throughout the house because you got some the night before. And every morning I woke up vomiting and pregnant with your child. I was always pregnant with your child. You were a terrible father!

"So what do you think?" Meme asks, flicking ash onto the floor.

"I think somebody needs to help her," I say. "It sounded to me like she is really being abused. I think she's telling the truth."

"About my letter?" Meme snaps, slapping the paper out of my hand.

"I think I'm nauseous," I say.

Meme reaches her hand into the Sex Victim Kit and pulls out the white envelope that has a stamp on it. She inserts the letter, licks the flap, seals it. I find the remote control and turn on the television.

On the screen, a midget in a baggy harlequin outfit is juggling three oranges. Over the midget's shoulder I recognize the front of Meme's parents' house. It cuts to Mr. Howard. He removes a fat brown cigar from his mouth.

"Welcome to *Bill Howard's 60 Minute Special*," Mr. Howard says.

A close-up of Meme's father looking like his face has been dragged over pavement is spliced with another scene of Meme's parents' house. A dozen policemen are kicking Meme's father in the teeth, the gut, and the balls while he squeals. Hundreds of people are gathered around the cops, shouting: "Rapist!"; "Swine!"; "Baby-killer!"

The screen switches to more footage. A woman with long blonde hair and a bubblegum-commercial-smile is carrying Meme's younger sister out of the house.

"The children were saved from this environment of abuse by Carol Porter," says a voice-over. "If you or anyone you know has been abused or is being abused, please call the Carol Porter Abuse Hotline. Crisis counselors are standing by to take your calls."

The Abuse Hotline number appears at the bottom of the screen.

Meme squats down on the floor with her arms wrapped around herself, rocking back and forth. I look back at the TV screen. It cuts to Meme's little brother, Edward, in handcuffs; he's being hauled into a black van by five oversized cops.

A mug-shot of Meme's father appears, his face broken and scabbed. I can barely make out the distorted features. His nose and mouth are beaten to a bloody pulp, missing his front teeth. His eyes are black and swollen shut. Meme covers her eyes.

"My father's in jail," Meme says. "I'm safe, now."

"…Carol Porter was tipped off about the abuse when Meme Lamb recovered repressed memories of her father molesting her…"

A photograph of Meme appears on the TV screen. She's posing in her white fur coat, ivory cigarette holder in hand. At the bottom of the screen, in neon yellow letters, is my home phone number.

"…The grandparents are also suspects and are being held in lockdown until they can prove that they are not involved in the orgiastic enterprise that has plagued the Lamb household…"

Footage of Meme's nearly crippled grandparents tangled in wires and electronic anklets flashes on the screen. The broadcast cuts to agents in black suits removing specs of dust with tweezers, then cuts to agents carrying articles of clothing out of the house where they place them into boxes.

"Bill Howard's Reality TV will continue with a live report! 24 hours a day! 7 days a week!" Mr. Howard says, "to keep the public updated as the investigation continues! Welcome, once again, to *Bill Howard's 60 Minute Special!* The subject of the hour will be the Penile Plethysmograph! An instrument used to determine sexual deviancy in pedophiles! We will meet the lab technicians who administered the test to Mr. Lamb! They will discuss the procedure and talk about Mr. Lamb's test results! And we will show video clips of the examination! So don't go away! Don't miss *Bill Howard's 60 Minute Special!* We'll be right back after these messages!"

An eerie piece of music introduces footage of Mr. Lamb; he is being pushed in a wheelchair down a red carpeted aisle by White Coats as he moves toward the camera. A white dog muzzle masks his face, and his head is held up by an aluminum brace. His wrists and ankles are fastened down in metal restraints. His hands are bleeding from the clamps that cut into his skin. And it looks like his fingers are taped together. He is lifted up onto a stage facing a large screen. Behind him, lab technicians set up a film projector.

I look at Meme, but I have to turn my head and look away. On the end table, in a frame, is a picture of Meme standing on the roof. She has a cup of coffee in one hand and a cigarette in the other. Her hair is ratted, messy and sexy. She is wearing my black coat over a white nightgown, as elegant as the one that she is wearing now. I took the picture one morning when we had breakfast on the roof of my building. That was the first week we met. It is a picture of a girl being herself, not striking a pose. It is a picture of a woman trying to figure things out. And in this picture, at the very least, it's done with a smile.

I don't know what to do. I pick up the phone and dial 911.

"*The Greatest Show on Earth*," a woman says.

I hang up the phone, try again.

"*The Greatest Show on Earth*," the woman says. "How can I help you?"

"You've got to be kidding?" I ask.

"No," she says. "I'm not kidding. We've been expecting your call."

I look closely at the walls. They are peppered with holes.

"Why would you be expecting my call?" I ask.

"You need help," she says. "You need someone to talk to."

"No," I say. "I don't need help. My girlfriend. My *ex*-girlfriend needs help. She's..."

"She's fine," the woman says. "She's doing everything she's supposed to do."

"She's doing everything she's supposed to?" I ask.

I stretch the telephone cord to the closet where I find a roll of duct-tape in a box on the floor.

"Yes," she says. "And so are you. Your reaction is perfectly natural. The show is progressing along quite smoothly."

"Quite smoothly, huh?" I say, tearing off a long strip of duct-tape.

"Yes," she says.

I put the duct-tape over several holes in the walls. Strip after strip, crisscrossing each other.

"So this is business as usual?" I ask. "Meme's got diarrhea of the mouth, her family is being torn apart, and I'm freaking out. This is what you call natural?"

I attach another strip of duct-tape. It's the end of the roll.

"Yes," she says, "you could put it like that."

"Well, what if I remove the cameras?" I ask. "What if I destroy them? What then?"

"Isn't that what those strips of duct-tape are all about?" she asks. "Don't bother. There are too many. Your apartment is painted with them. They are the size of needles. You would have to tear the place apart to get them all out."

"Can you see me right now?" I ask.

"Well, of course," she says.

"Do you see this?" I ask. "What am I doing?"

"Right now, you are giving me the finger."

"That's right," I say. "Think of this as a big Fuck You!"

I hang up the phone and pick up the picture of Meme. I pace about the room.

"Do you remember when we danced to Frank Sinatra?" I ask. "Do you remember that night?"

On the TV, another Meme. She sits there and stares at herself.

"Look at this picture," I say. "This isn't a woman who was tortured at a Satanic ritual. This isn't a woman who was gang raped or abducted by aliens. This isn't a woman who was raped by her father. Look at this picture."

She glances vacantly at the picture, then turns back to the TV.

"How common is sex abuse?" a voice-over asks.

"Three out of four women are sexually abused," an expert says. "Though I think it's higher than that."

I pull Meme's head back by her hair. I hold the picture to her face, up to her eyes, pressing the frame against her nose.

"Look at this picture," I say.

Pressed so closely, it's all she can see. But she doesn't even recognize herself.

"You are hurting me," she says.

I let go of her head and walk across the room; I flip through the record albums on a shelf next to the stereo. I find Frank Sinatra's Greatest Hits and put it on the record player.

Frank Sinatra's "All of Me" comes on.

"Studies have shown that…"

I turn up the volume on the stereo.

"Remember this song?" I ask. "Remember when we danced to this song? Remember when we used to do things like go out to dinner or lay in bed for hours? Remember your childhood, all the stories you told me about being on the Little League basketball and softball team. And when you told your parents you didn't like playing sports, they said you didn't have to. And when you said you wanted to study music, they bought you a piano, and paid for lessons, several lessons a week, for the next five years. And your favorite thing as a child—singing in the choir. Where did you find the time for rehearsal when you were being shuttled out to space by aliens every day? Or held captive in a snake pit for months?"

I can see her trying to think, to suspend disbelief.

Her picture appears on the TV screen. It's not the same one used in the Hotline infomercials. She smiles.

They are watching, I think to myself. This is very clever. Mr. Howard is listening to everything I'm saying. He's controlling her emotions. And then I realize. We are 'Live'; we are on television.

"Meme," I say. "Remember this song?"

Meme moves her hand in front of the TV. She reaches out and touches the screen. I run to the closet to find a baseball bat, knowing that I don't even own one. I find a broom in the kitchen. I try a practice swing, but it's too lightweight. The only thing I can find is a frying pan. It is silent in the other room. When I return, I understand why. Meme is experiencing stage fright. Or she has fallen in love.

I bring the frying pan down hard on the front edge of the TV set. It sends the image scrambling in black and white stripes, then flashes like the flash of a camera. It turns black.

"You hit me," Meme says, pointing at the television. "You hit me in the face."

"And now I'm going to break your leg," I say.

I swing the frying pan hard into the screen; it nearly disappears into the TV.

CHAPTER 8

▼

THE WOMEN'S SUPPORT GROUP

This morning Mr. Howard signed a six month lease on the space at the Paris Theater. It was the largest space available. We first checked out a basement in an old church but it was too small and besides, Mr. Howard said, "I don't like the idea of being right under the feet of our major competitors!"

I was a little put off by the history of the location. Over the years it has attracted groupies of Rock 'n' Roll bands that bite the heads off of rats, bikers dressed in black leather for kinky S&M fetish shows, and university students on mushrooms who would trip out on the absurd theatrical performances.

I told him this setup may threaten the integrity of my services.

"You're looking at it the wrong way!" Mr. Howard said. "We'll be able to connect with a whole new population of people! It's like we are missionaries traveling to unknown lands! Reaching out! Spreading the word of your gospel to an indigent community of an unenlightened people! A group of confused youngsters just out for a good time will swing by the theater and, for a reasonable fee, have their lives transformed by the experience of your services! Think about the justice in that! They'll get to knock off two birds with one stone: the desire to amuse themselves to death, and a covert philosophical education—answers to the big questions and a twelve-step program to the good life! Discrimination is bad for business. We need to embrace everyone if the meek of the earth are going to come to us, pay the fee, and gain salvation!"

Mr. Howard pointed out the distinguished texture of the layout. Soft red velvet chairs in rows that slope up toward the back to allow all audience members a clear view. The seven-hundred-square-foot stage made of dark antique wood. Red velvet curtains that hang from the three-story-high ceiling. Beautiful black and white Italian tiles that checker the auditorium floor with red runners rolled down the two main aisles. Mr. Howard said that his film crew could capture some captivating angle shots from the opera booths that are on both sides and along the back of the theater.

My seminar certificate is the last thing I pack into my box of belongings. Mr. Howard told me to leave the furniture and bookshelf behind, he'll send some garbage men over later to haul it all out to the dump. He knows an interior decorator who specializes in office design and has even worked on a few productions in Hollywood.

I carry my box out to my old station wagon, glance one last time at the dilapidated building, then get in the car and drive to the Paris Theater. Mr. Howard has come up with a rigorous schedule demanding appointments with each of my clients several times a week and possibly a support group session every other day.

And Mr. Howard came up with the idea for the MPD 500 race. The first client to get five hundred personalities will win a free trip to Disneyland and a teddy bear. Mr. Howard said this would be an incentive to get my clients to the theater and hasten the healing process. He has offered to provide transportation for Meme to ensure her attendance.

On a billboard in front of the Paris Theater is a sign:

BILL HOWARD
PRESENTS
CAROL'S PSYCHOLOGICAL SERVICES

Arched above the entrance to the theater is a sign in neon lights that reads "THE GATES OF HELP."

The doors open automatically. I walk past the ticket booth and popcorn machine and through the red drapery which leads to the red carpeted aisle dividing the columns of red velvet chairs.

Mr. Howard's interior decorator has furnished the stage with a red velvet chaise lounge that Meme is reclining on, her head resting on the headrest. My other clients are sitting and playing with toys and stuffed animals on a huge gold Oriental rug.

Meme is in costume: an elegant red dress curves across her body. She has a black boa around her neck and long black gloves that stretch from her fingers up her arm above her elbow.

A dark wood antique desk is off-center to the left of the stage with a well-padded leather chair behind it. Another chair is in front of the desk, angled toward the front of the stage. A few women wearing light brown tunics, with black CPS armbands around their biceps, reposition the desk.

Mr. Howard has added a black chimney hat and a white cane to his trademark black tuxedo image, something he tells me that he found in the back storage.

"Cha-cha," Mr. Howard says, dancing his round body down the steps, twirling the cane around his white-cuffed wrist. He takes the tall black hat off his head and bows, conducting his white cane in the direction of the stage. "What do you think?"

"I can't believe it," I say. "Is this really happening?"

"This is only the beginning!" Mr. Howard says.

His mouth spreads across his face, revealing his gums and yellow teeth.

"We need to present ourselves as a respectable establishment!" Mr. Howard says. "I have hired a few assistants. They are mostly for dramatic effect but they are at your service. They can help guarantee that your clients make it to their appointments. Cheap too! I found a couple of them working at a burger joint, the others were standing outside the unemployment office. And look!" Mr. Howard points at a bookshelf full of books titled *The Malleus Porculorum*. "I have printed a new edition of your self-help book: *The Malleus Porculorum*. That's *The Pigs' Hammer* translated into Latin. The title, not the book. It kind of sounds like some medical term. A distinguished sound to it. The right element, I believe, for a credible bestseller."

The self-help books are priced at twenty-five dollars. There's also a new edition of the coloring workbook.

"I don't know how to thank you," I say.

"You can start by getting to work immediately!" Mr. Howard says. He flips the black hat through the air and onto his head. "Time is money!"

"Shouldn't we wait for Pinhead and Stump?" I ask.

Mr. Howard points his cane to the back of the auditorium. I look up at the opera booths. In the center I see Pinhead waving from behind his camera and Stump flickering the spotlight on and off, his afro glowing behind the chrome spotlight. I wave back at them.

"Now get up there!" Mr. Howard says, pushing me toward the stage.

I walk up the steps to the stage.

"May I have your attention, please?" I ask. "Please put the toys down. Listen up."

Meme uncrosses her legs and stands up off the chaise longue. I lead her to the center of the gold rug. Stump's spotlight radiates her face.

"Ladies, we have a new victim today!" I announce to the incest survivors, clapping my hands together. "Her name is Meme!"

I put my arms around Meme and hold her for a few seconds while the other survivors cheer, whistle, and shake their bodies on the rug, creaking the structure of the building.

"Welcome," I say, spreading my arms, "to our circle of healing and empowerment."

The women calm down and form a circle, opening up a space for Meme. I take Meme's hand and help her sit down on the rug. All the survivors stare at her with awkward, constipated smiles.

"Let's all introduce ourselves," I say, turning to Michelle. "Michelle, why don't you start."

Michelle pushes both her hands into her crotch, a nervous habit caused by incest.

"My name is Michelle and I was raped by my..."

"Next," Mr. Howard says.

Michelle cries on her sleeve. Bozanne, who is sitting next to her, rubs Michelle's back.

"My name is Bozanne," she continues to rub Michelle's back. "I have fifty personalities now and I eat a lot because my daddy made sex with me all the time when I was a little girl and he was a High Priest in the Satanic Cult and I was tortured and raped by The Cult and sold as a prostitute..."

"Next," Mr. Howard cuts her off, yawns.

"Hi, I'm Betty and I feel like I'm the only one who wasn't molested," she cries with her head between her knees, digging her fingernails into her thick brown hair, a white bow on top. She looks like a twenty-year-old dressed in a little Catholic school girl's uniform.

"Little Betty doesn't have her memories yet, but we are working on them," I say, shrugging at Betty. I turn toward Meme. "Betty is new, too, Meme. She has been in the group for two weeks." I roll my eyes. "Betty, you hurt the whole group when you withhold your traumatic stories." Little Betty pulls her knees up to her chest and cries with her head down. "Sally has been here as long as you and she already has seven personalities." I look around at the entire group. "Sally is a good group-thinker, isn't she? Let's give her a round of applause."

The whole group flies into a thunderous roar, rattling the stage floor and chandeliers. There are high-pitched howls, hyena-like cackles, piercing whistles. Betty scratches her arms.

"But I'm *trying* to remember," Betty says. "I'm trying..."

"Next," I say. "Sally the group-thinker is next!"

"Hi, I'm Sally," she says, "and I have seven personalities in only two weeks and I was molested by my daddy and he sacrificed my pet rabbit at a Satanic ritual and he always did me...I remember him doing me when I was four weeks old and he never stopped and he gave it to me everyday until I was twenty-one years old and my grandpa used to give me candy and make me suck on him and he did that since I was two weeks old." She lifts her arms which are covered in blood stained bandages from wrist to shoulder. "I must be getting a lot better because I've cut myself over thirty times this week!"

Another round of applause combined with stomping.

"I cut myself, too," another survivor says, waving her swollen arms in the air.

The survivors turn toward one another, displaying the cuts on their arms and wrists, talking passionately about their wounds and near-death experiences.

Meme opens a silver case and picks out several capsules, plops them in her mouth.

"Self-mutilation will make you feel better," I say, looking at Meme. "It's part of the healing process. As long as it doesn't go too far."

"Next!" Mr. Howard yells.

The rest of the women in the circle talk about how they were raped by their fathers. They give out the number of their personalities. They talk about how they were Satanic priestess until they met me and broke the cycle.

"What about you, Meme?" one woman asks. "Tell us your traumatic story."

Meme is dozing off from the medication, her head swinging about like it's connected to a swivel. She lifts the red strap up to her shoulder and collapses into the soft cushion of Bozanne's body. Bozanne holds her up. Hands that look like extra-large mittens grope Meme's face and clumsily push her red hair back out of her eyes. She is practically brain dead from the meds. I'll have to give her something to counteract the stupor before she slips into a coma.

"I don't know," Meme says, slowly. "I don't remember..."

"Don't you have a Candy Man story?" Sally asks. "We all have Candy Man stories. Haven't you read the book?"

"I don't know what happened," Meme says, wiping her nose with the back of her black glove.

"Come on," Bozanne says. "Tell us about the man who gave you candy for some pussy."

"Yeah, tell us what he did."

"You have to tell us..."

"Just do it! Meme! You can do it!"

"You're not supposed to keep it from the group," I say. "You have to re-experience the trauma if you want to get better."

"Well," Meme says, "I have some memories."

Stump's spotlight zeroes in on Meme's face.

"Yeessss?" the group says.

"But they are," Meme puts her head down, "fuzzy."

Stump gives me the attention of his spotlight.

"Meme," I say, leaning my upper body forward while sitting down on the gold rug with my legs folded in, "from here on out, you need to spend every waking moment dealing with your issues. In a support group environment you get to hear the traumatic stories of other victims and after hearing them over and over you will eventually develop your own, although very similar, traumatic stories. Most of your memories of abuse are stored in your multiple personalities which you haven't yet discovered. When you were raped and molested by your father, you became fragmented by splitting into different personalities so that you could survive the abuse. One personality may have the memory of the time you were forced to have sex with a corpse. Another personality may store all the memories of the times you were forced to perform special favors for your dad's bridge partners. You need to retrieve all of these memories in order to become whole again. It's a life-long struggle but I practice techniques which effectively provoke my clients to remember the most unbelievable things. Eventually, your memories of sex abuse that seem blurry and dubious, even *fuzzy*, will become so vivid, so crystal clear, you will actually begin to feel like you are re-experiencing the rape all over again. When the memories feel this real, then you know you're getting better."

I stand up and open my arms out toward the group.

"Ladies," I say, "let's have a Hate Session. Everybody get into Hate Therapy position."

The survivors rock back and forth, giggling and slapping their tummies. I walk toward Meme, extending a hand.

"Meme," I pull Meme up, "you need to sit at the center of the circle. Bozanne, you should be with her. You should sit behind her and comfort her so she knows that she is with someone who is safe. In a Hate Therapy session we reenact situations that you experienced while growing up. It involves role playing. You need to confront the truth in order to deal with it. In this case you will sit at the center of the circle and we will treat you the way your parents treated you and this will help you remember what your childhood was like."

"My memories are so vague," Meme says. "I can't really remember. I don't think anything happened."

"Give it time," I say. "Just give it time and the memories will come raining down on you. That's what I'm here for."

"Whatever pops into your mind is a fact," Bozanne adds.

I slip my arm around Meme's thin waist and walk her to the center of the circle. Bozanne struggles onto her feet and walks over to a prop bin in the back of the stage and returns with a medium-sized pillow. Meme sits down and holds the pillow against her stomach. Bozanne, squishing like a waterbed, sits down behind Meme. The support group circle constricts around them.

"You are bad," I yell to get the game started.

Meme pushes back into the sea of Bozanne.

"You are a bad girl," my clients chant.

"You are my sexual plaything!" Sally says. "Your mama doesn't love you. Your papa wants to play with you."

Meme sinks into Bozanne's valleys; she squeezes the pillow and twists her head from side to side.

"Please stop!" Meme cries.

The survivors pace in front of Meme.

"Bad...bad...bad," they say.

They loom and plunge down on Meme, digging their nails into her bony arms.

"Your mother wants to kill you."

"Your mom and daddy hate you."

"Your father wants to eat you."

Betty runs to the back of the stage and covers her eyes with her hands and cries.

"You are a harlot," Sally says, poking her fingers all over Meme. "You are a sex toy!"

The women leap and stretch over each other to get a piece. Stump dims the spotlight, darkening the bodies and faces panting on the stage in a tribal ritual. I hear someone delivering blows to the pillow as if punching a punching bag. I hear Meme choking as if being strangled. Then I see Sally's hand extend above the crowd holding a tuft of Meme's hair. That's when I say enough is enough. I order everyone to lay off.

But Sally won't stop.

"Your mom and dad want to rape you," Sally says. "They want to beat you."

She climbs over Meme, trying to push her dress over her head.

I order Sally to stop, this time louder, but she continues to grope and fondle Meme's body. Bozanne and Michelle pull at Sally's legs and drag her across the stage as she screams out in a murderous rage.

The other women back away, spread apart. Meme turns over, gasping for air. She is scratched, bruised, and laying in mounds of her own spit and hair.

"Now let's have a Love Therapy Session," I say, holding Meme in my arms. "Show Meme what her new family is like. Let her know how much you love her."

All at once the women close in on Meme. They pet her face and tell her that they love her, she is a good girl, they will protect her.

"Everything is going to be okay," my clients say.

"It's not your fault, Meme," Bozanne says, wrapping her bloated arms around Meme. "It's not your fault!"

"It's not your fault!" I say, holding Meme's shoulders, staring into her eyes. "It's not your fault."

"It's not your fault!" Betty cries from the back of the stage.

"It's not your fault!" Michelle adds.

"It's not your fault!" Mr. Howard hollers.

"We are your new family, Meme." I gently hold Meme's hand. "And we all love you."

Mr. Howard tells everyone to take five. During the break, the women pat Meme on the back and congratulate each other. Betty crawls off to a corner where she holds her knees to her chest and shivers like a frightened animal.

Mr. Howard wants me to begin the MPD 500 race right away.

"I have already made the posters," Mr. Howard says, unrolling a large sheet of paper.

In big yellow letters:

BILL HOWARD
PRESENTS
CAROL'S CHILDREN
AND
THE DAMSEL'S CHORUS OF DISTRESS
Experience Meme Lamb And Her Chorus Of A Thousand Personalities!

Come See Bozanne, A Two-Year-Old Baby Girl The Size Of A Locomotive!
Meet The Reincarnation Of Napoleon, Joan Of Arc, And Louis XIV!

"One thousand personalities?" I ask.

"Originally, I was thinking five thousand!" Mr. Howard says, sniffing a new cigar. "I thought a thousand was more realistic. Now, please don't pester me with your self-doubt. You'll be surprised by what you can do if you just put your mind to it. And if I were you, I would start doing just that. We don't have time to lose."

Mr. Howard lights his cigar, walks away from me and across the stage, and down the steps to the front row where he sits in one of the soft red velvet chairs.

I try to get everybody's attention so we can move right along to the next stage in the healing process: the MPD 500 race.

"May I have your attention?" I ask. "Quiet down, victims, come on, pay attention. Gather around in a healing circle."

My clients all return to their positions and form a human circle, holding hands with one another.

"Okay, thank you, thank you," I say. "You are being such good survivors today. Okay. Who wants to go to Disneyland?"

"Me," the survivors roar together.

"The first client to reach five hundred personalities wins the MPD 500," I say. "Whoever wins gets a free trip to Disneyland and a free teddy-bear."

"Disneyland!" they shout and bloat with smiles.

"Disneyland," I yell back at them.

"Disneyland," they wiggle anxiously for the race to begin.

I turn to Meme, who is looking somewhat confused.

"Meme," I say, stepping into the center of the circle, "the MPD 500 is a race to see who can get five hundred new personalities the fastest. Who knows, you might have what it takes to be an MPD 500 champ your first week in the group!"

The MPD 500 race is off to a lightning speed beginning; there's an unruffled contagion effect purling around the healing circle.

Sally announces that her name is Anne Frank. Even Betty conforms and the two of them go on and on about the Nazis dragging them off to be gassed.

"I'm also Anne Frank," Bozanne says.

"Hoo-hoo!" Mr. Howard howls from the front row.

Stump's spotlight slowly moves around the circle.

It's too good to be true.

"I've been in the dark for two years," Bozanne cries. "Why can't I go out and play with the other children?"

"I'm Anne Frank," Michelle says. "I'm Anne Frank!"

And then Meme ruins everything.

"Hello," I say, "Meme! Is anybody home? It's your turn, Meme!"

Stump's spotlight shines on Meme's face. Her complexion turns a fluorescent white.

Meme slowly lifts her head up from between her knees and looks out at the healing circle.

"Meme," I say, "come on, get your act together. The MPD 500 race started five minutes ago!"

"I'm…trying," Meme mumbles.

"Everybody else is Anne Frank right now," I say, becoming agitated.

"I don't…know," Meme says, trying to keep her eyes open.

"Come on, Meme!" Bozanne shouts.

"Meme, don't you want to be Anne Frank like everybody else?" Sally pushes her.

"Get it together," I beg. "Please?"

"What are you doing here?" Michelle asks, "if you're not going to participate…"

"Meme," Mr. Howard speaks softly from his front row seat, "don't you want to be the winner of the MPD 500?"

Meme pushes her hands over her face and cries. She puts her head back down between her legs. Mr. Howard stands up in the front row.

"Come on," Mr. Howard says. Tears in his eyes, he says, "Don't you want to be a survivor?"

Meme covers her ears with her black feathered boa and howls out in a long, dreadful cry, her eyes lit up by Stump's spotlight. Her hands are squeezed into fists. Her face is blood-vessel blue. Meme opens her swollen pink mouth and wails:

"I'm Anne Frank!"

The words echo throughout the auditorium. Mr. Howard's face becomes animated with joy. He points his finger at Pinhead to roll the camera. The red light starts blinking. We are 'Live' on television.

"I was raped by my father!" Meme says, slamming her fists down on the floor. Spit flies out of her mouth. "I was raped by my mother!"

Mr. Howard lets out a silent "Whoo-hoo!"

CHAPTER 9

ANOTHER DAY, ANOTHER ALTER

"Hi, I'm Anne Frank!" Meme says.

I'm standing at the door, holding it open. Meme is missing a shoe, which causes her to stand lopsided in the hallway outside my apartment. There are bald patches on her scalp, and white gauze is taped around her left wrist with Sylvester and Tweety Band-Aids.

"And I'm Lord Byron," I say.

"Please help me," Meme says. "May I hide here for a little while?"

"Meme," I say, "are you going fucking crazy?"

What am I thinking? She's already crazy.

"Please?" Meme asks. "My name is Anne Frank. I have nowhere else to go. Please let me come in?"

Meme is holding several new books in one arm and a couple of shopping bags in the other. I suck hard on my cigarette, burning my throat.

"Meme, this is starting to really freak me out," I say.

"My name is Anne…"

"Sorry, sorry," I say. "Anne, sorry about that." Smoke slowly crawls out of my mouth. "This is kind of weird, don't you think? I mean, it's a nice midsummer evening. We could do anything. We could go for a walk, have a quiet dinner someplace."

"Are you trying to get me killed? The Nazis will torture and gas me. I'll become a subject in one of their morbid laboratory experiments. Please, I don't mean to cause any trouble. I'll be quiet. I'll stay in your attic."

"I don't have an attic," I say. "Check with my neighbor. Or down the block. This is an apartment. Good luck."

I begin to shut the door.

"Please, I beg you," Meme says, stretching her red mouth through the crack of the door. "What if he's a Nazi?" She pouts her big lips. "What if he rapes and kills me?"

The word *rape* bothers me. Because I might be on television. I might look insensitive. My neighbor isn't a Nazi. I don't know what he is. That's what worries me. I can't let Meme roam the streets in this condition. This is pitiful.

"I promise I'll be real quiet," Meme says. "I'm just really scared and I need a place to stay. I don't know where else to go…"

"Come in," I surrender.

I put my cigarette out and light another. I intentionally let the smoke sting my eyes. I pull the blinds up, about to open a window to ventilate some air, when I hear:

"Close the window! Close the fucking window! Are you trying to get me killed!"

I rip at the blinds several times until they clatter down the window and block out the evening sun.

"Thank you," Meme says. "Thank you. I'll be real quiet. I promise not to get in the way. You are so kind."

"Meme," I say. "I mean, sorry, Anne, uh…"

I nod my head and take a hard drag.

"What is your name?" she asks.

"My name?"

"Yes," she says. "What is your name? Who are you?"

"Frank," I say, smiling, extending my box of cigarettes. "Would you like a cigarette?"

"Oh, no," Anne Frank says. "I don't smoke."

I laugh a quiet, painful laugh.

Why couldn't she come home as a bohemian French girl or something? With a few major adjustments, we could have something pretty good going. If I have to dig at the bottom of a quagmire, I may as well dig for gold.

"Do you mind if I use your bathroom?" Anne Frank asks. "I could really use a shower."

"Sure," I say. "Yeah, go ahead."

She stands there. She doesn't move. She looks confused.

"I'm sorry," she says, "but where is the bathroom?"

"It's where you spend most of your time looking at yourself!" I say. "Don't ask me, 'Where's the fucking bathroom?'"

"I don't understand you," she says.

"I don't understand *you*," I say. "You can find my apartment, but you can't find the bathroom?"

"You are hurting my feelings," she says.

She covers her mouth with both hands.

"I burned all of your clothes today," I say, testing her knowledge about the location of the closet.

Meme drops the books and shopping bags. Gift boxes and self-help books litter the floor: *Return to Infancy*; *Satanic Ritual Abuse and You!*; *Merging Personalities*. There is also what looks like the 2nd Edition to *The Pigs' Hammer*. It's called *The Malleus Porculorum*. Apparently, it comes with a coloring book.

Meme runs toward the closet and opens the door. She scrapes the hangers across the metal rod, caresses the fabric of her dresses, and pants into the sleeve of her mink coat.

"So I see that you can find the closet," I say.

I almost tell her that I trashed all of her makeup, but she is already on the verge of going postal. I should have known better than to tease her about her wardrobe. That's like telling Heloise that Abelard is a goner.

She takes the mink coat off the hanger and hugs it to her chest while walking to the bathroom. The human tornado routine thrashes once again in there, a tantrum far more violent than any other. The joke about her clothes was hitting below the belt. It just might push her over the edge of a razor, then I would have a dead girl on my hands and a lot of explaining to do to the TV viewers. It would be indirect murder. "Man Kills Girl by Threatening Versace Dress with Scissors."

I ram my shoulder into the door but it won't open.

"Meme," I yell at the wooden door, "let me in!"

I push my shoulder into the door again, causing a pain to travel through my arm, up my spine, buckling my knees. The door opens.

Meme is wearing the mink coat and staring at her reflection.

"Meme," I say, "what is going on?"

Meme touches her face with her hands and then stares with awe at the Sylvester and Tweety bandages on her wrist. She peels off a bandage and several tiny slits in her wrist puss and bleed the smallest little dewdrops of blood. I stare at Meme's face reflected in the shattered pieces of mirror still hanging above the bathroom sink.

"Meme," I say, "I think you should be committed, for your own safety. I'm concerned. Please don't be insulted. But I think you need some serious help. And from what I see, you're not getting any. We had an agreement. You were going to put an end to all of this. You were going to tell the truth and quit this bullshit."

Hands with long chipped fingernails push into the reflection of Meme's breasts.

"My presents!" Meme says. "I want to open my presents!"

Meme hurries out to where she dropped her shopping bags. A fly buzzes in circles and I take a swipe at it, but miss. It flies frantically into the wall, like fingers tapping, then swoops at me. I deliver several punches into the air and chase the fly out of the bathroom to where Meme is smiling giddily, opening up a present like a five-year-old on Christmas morning. Several presents have already been opened. A blue and red laser gun is on the floor along side a Jack in the Box. Four Barbie dolls lay on top of each other, tangled in a stiff orgy. She tears the gold wrapping off of another box and pulls out a Malcolm X mask with black glasses over the eye holes.

"What in the hell are you going to do with this stuff?" I ask her.

Meme holds the Malcolm X mask to her face.

"We must fight against oppression!" Meme says through the Malcolm X mouth hole, then drops the mask on the floor and unties a white bow on the red gift-wrap of another present.

She scratches the paper and lifts the lid off of the box. There's a rattle, a milk bottle, and a pacifier.

"What?" I ask. "Are you pregnant?"

She opens up another box.

"I want to know what you are planning on doing with all of this junk," I say. "Where did you get it? And what the fuck are you going to do with it?"

"Mr. Howard gave me these presents," Meme says. She puts the pacifier in her mouth and then pulls it out. "The costumes are for role playing. By acting out different roles and situations, I become acquainted with those aspects of my self that have experienced abuse and oppression. I have experienced some horrible things, and not just in this life. The toys are to help me get in touch with my inner child. To regain the innocence I had before I was corrupted by a life of injustices and inequality. Before I was violated."

"You have toiled no more than the lilies of the field," I say. "What are you talking about? A chipped fingernail lands you in the emergency room! You have a silver spoon in your mouth. You haven't worked a day in your life. And you are trying to pawn yourself off like you've been in slave labor? Like you understand what it means to be a black man with a noose around his neck? This is twisted. I'm sorry to inform you of this, but just because every whim of yours cometh not on a silver platter doesn't mean that you suffer terribly, like Jews in a Nazi concentration camp or an African-American about to hang. Meme, this isn't therapy!"

"I'm already a star," Meme says. "You're just jealous, full of envy, spite! I'm a celebrity!"

"I'm the fat lady singing," I say. "Please, if you want to be the local idiot, I have no doubt whatsoever of your ability to perform the role superbly. It suits you quite well."

I pick through the dirty clothes pile until I find a shirt that doesn't have a pungent odor. Since things have fallen apart, I haven't had time to wash a load. I put on my black dress shoes. Meme stands in front of the mirror, trying on Halloween masks, courtesy of Mr. Howard.

"Where are you going?" Meme asks.

"I'm going to work!" I say. "Do any of your alternate personalities have jobs? Maybe like Cara the Construction Worker? Or Jenny the Janitor? Or how about, Hannah the House Cleaner? Or are they all dead martyrs or from the land of make-believe? Idols of worship and praise?"

Meme sits down in her vanity chair and unwraps a handful of white tissue paper. She holds up a glass slipper and asks:

"Will you help me try this on?"

I called the temp agency about getting some work today. Anything, I said. I would clean outhouses, I would handle rodents, I would dig graves. Anything is better than this.

With the temp agency you have to call in regularly if you want to stay on their list for job referrals. The girl on the phone put me on notice because I haven't called for the past few days. Another absence without calling in and they will have to let me go. She wasn't very sympathetic when I told her that I've been helping my girlfriend deal with her issues. I gave her the entire run of excuses. I have been trying to protect my girlfriend from the sex-ring, I said, they are coming after her. She is wanted. I'm sure you have heard of her. She's all over the news. The one with the fur coat striking a pose? That's my girlfriend! "You wish," she said.

At my temp job I'm holding a phone to my head, pretending that I'm in the middle of a political survey with someone somewhere. I'm doing everything I can to keep from dropping my head down on the table and taking a nap. My boss has been watching me all evening long, so I've been calling the numbers. Strange, all the people sound like the same person. I try to appear busy when he walks by and stares at my sleepless eyes, my nervous hands that twitch. He's holding a Chinese take-out carton and an article from some newspaper.

"Will you ask Meme to sign this?" he asks. "Will you get her autograph?"

It's a cover story about Meme. I look up at him and nod. He walks away, smiling, and then steps into the break-room to eat his dinner.

I dial Paul and Amber's phone number.

"*The Greatest Show on Earth*," a woman answers.

The same thing happened on my way to work when I called from a pay phone.

I hang up and sit there silently for several minutes. I try calling 911.

"*The Greatest Show on Earth*," says the operator.

"Fuck," I say. "It's you again."

"Can I help you?" the woman asks.

"Yes," I say. "I have an emergency."

"Police, fire or medical?" she asks.

"I don't know," I say. "It's just an emergency situation. I need to call outside this place. Can you get me in touch with someone on the outside? Someone is being harmed."

"One moment," she says.

A minute passes.

"Medical," the same woman says. "How can I help you?"

"It's still you," I say.

"Yes," she says.

"Then why did you ask if I wanted the police, the fire department, or medical?"

"I think that's a reasonable question," she says.

"It would be if you were going to transfer me to one of them," I say.

"Well, why don't you tell me more about what kind of a situation you've got there," she says.

"I've got an emergency situation," I say. "I don't know who to call. I just don't want to be a part of this anymore. I agreed to be on this show, I know. So please don't tell me that. I know I signed the papers, but I want to be let go. Can you help me with that? Can you get me in touch with a real person?"

"Well," the woman says, "I'm a real person."

"I know," I say. "I'm not saying that you aren't real."

"So what's the problem?" she asks.

"I just told you," I say. "I agreed to be on this Reality TV show, and I can't get out."

"Why don't you just go home?" she asks.

"Because it's there too," I say with hostility. "It's everywhere. You know this already."

"What's there?" she asks. "What's everywhere? Reality?"

"Yes," I say. "No. Unreality."

"You feel like your home is unreal?"

"Yes," I say.

"Why?" she asks. "Did you do something to it? Did you change it? What could you do to your home to make it unreal? I'm curious to know how reality becomes unreality without altering any part of it."

"You add false elements," I say. "You substitute the initial conditions with fictions. You distort personal histories. For example, you have my girlfriend thinking that she has multiple personalities and repressed memories. She looks the same, and, for the most part, her constitution is the same, but her function is not. Her meaning is not the same. And yes, I know, people change; they change all the time. We discover things about ourselves, we learn who we are, what we like, by the trials of real life. I want to fight the battle of real life, not some artificial one. Can you help me get there? And please don't tell me to go home. My home is no longer my home because its function is no longer a place to sleep, eat, and shit in peace. It is now a tv show. So, can you help me get back to reality? Where the human function, in my opinion, is to solve real problems, not create fake ones."

"But aren't fake problems just as integral to life as real problems?"

"No," I say. "And who cares? That's not my question."

"You call me for help," she says. "You say you have this problem. If I understand you correctly, your problem has to do with this world you've gotten yourself into. You signed a contract, you signed your life away. You say it's a fake, superficial, artificial world. And then you allude to this other world, this other dimension, and you say things are more real there. I wonder if that is really so, if you really mean it like that. Don't you think that, quite possibly, the two worlds you refer to are one and the same? That unreality is just as real as reality is unreal? That everything that happens, for whatever reason, for better or worse, is just the world you live in? A slice of life?"

"I would rather not think so," I say.

"You would rather not think so," she repeats. "Huh. You say that your life has been invaded by tv and therapy, as if this is a rare disease. Well, in the real world, life *is* tv and therapy. What makes you think that you should be treated differently? What makes you think that you are so special that you should be immune?"

"I'm not saying that I'm better than anybody," I say. "I just want things to be different. For life to have value."

"Well," she says. "Enough talk like that. Your life means one thing to you, and another thing to others. What does it matter? What is the harm? So yours is lived out before millions of viewers."

"It's a matter of respect," I say. "Respect for life. The truth should matter. It should have value."

"But isn't it the truth that things are the way they are?" she asks. "Whatever happens, happens. It is what it is. You can't do anything about it. Why bother? It sounds to me like you want to change reality, not the other way around."

"Maybe I do," I say. "Maybe I want life to be better than it is."

"Just like everyone else," she says.

"Yes," I say. "I guess so."

I am such a fool.

It is a crushing moment when you realize that you are a nobody. Your dreams only shine in the spotlight in your mind. It is humiliating when you look in the mirror just before walking out the door to the workplace that owns you. You stare at yourself and think: this is it? The possibilities are endless on the wide Hollywood screen: an infinite number of magically happy endings.

And this is it? This is the one I get?

I get home late; it is suspiciously quiet in the apartment. Meme is in bed, sleeping peacefully. But I don't buy it. On the dining table, the big book is open to a page about body memories. I take this as some kind of warning. The book explains: "That's when your body re-experiences the trauma." I'm tempted to skip to the last page to see how it all ends.

At about four in the morning, the body memories kick in.

Meme pounces about on the mattress—naked and spread-eagled—thrusting her hips toward the ceiling like a Playboy Bunny.

"Bad girl," Meme moans. "Bad...bad."

Her hands are behind her head, pinned down by an invisible figure. Her moan rises into a high pitched chant, full of heavy breathing and the promise of an early orgasm. But she goes on and on like it's a marathon. I get up and walk over to the bed and slap her across the face.

"Meme," I say. "Wake up. Wake up."

She crawls out of bed and flings herself onto the floor, humps the hardwoods.

"You're a nasty little girl," Meme vexes herself.

"Meme," I say, standing over her, trying to drag her back to the bed, trying to snap her out of it, "Meme…"

But it's useless. The spell can't be broken.

The screaming attracts several neighbors, and my landlord, to our door.

"Childhood…trauma," I tell the landlord.

He's standing in the hallway in his night gown, trying to look over my shoulder. I'm trying to block his view, miming his movements. Several neighbors in pajamas and slippers stand up on their tiptoes to look over his back. I look over my shoulder and see Meme humping an invisible being.

"Should I call the doctor?" he asks. "Is she going to be alright?"

"Yes," I say, waving him off. "I mean, no. Don't bother. I already called the doctor. Everything will be fine."

He just stands there, he's not walking away, he steps closer. I can hear Meme's bare ass smacking on the floor. There's a lot of grunting. I pat him on the shoulder and thank him for showing concern.

"Everything is going to be okay," I say, forcing a smile.

"I'm getting complaints," he says, "about the noise."

Meme howls, "Bad slut! Bad!"

"I'm real sorry about this," I say, and then without much confidence, "she's getting better…*really*."

"Try to keep it down," he says, peering over my shoulder. "It's past four in the morning."

I hear thrashing and banging. My landlord's face and body revolt with each crash.

"She needs my help," I say, closing the door, "I need to go…sorry about this…"

"The neighbors are trying to sleep," he says, as the door closes.

I want to tell him, "So am I."

Chapter 10

DENIAL

The Paris Theater is scented with bouquets of red flowers from love-struck fans. Meme has received at least a thousand 'Get Well' cards. The most mysterious gift came from Jane Rhino, the former Attorney General of the United States. It was a large wooden crate stamped with black letters: The Way Co. Project. It included a little card, which read: Save The Children. Yours, Jane Rhino. The crate contains tear gas and military-grade weaponry.

The donations for the Help Save Meme Fund have already topped a million dollars. Mr. Howard has sold out the second printing of *The Malleus Porculorum* by advertising the book on television. It's a little too much for him to handle right now so he's hooked up with an agent to negotiate a five-book deal with a major publishing house. These will be Feel Better books, he says. Vanity without the vanity press.

"That's where the money is these days," Mr. Howard said. "Anything that's not an opiate to the masses and their despair is guaranteed to make the slush pile."

Right now, the only thing standing between me and my wildest dreams is Mr. and Mrs. Lamb's youngest daughter. This is a serious problem, especially with *Bill Howard's Reality TV Law & Order* just around the corner. Jill claims that her father never touched her. It's not going to look so good when she takes the stand and says, "I love my Daddy!"

In the Paris Theater, Jill is sitting in a wooden chair, center-stage, her pink dress barely hanging on her body. Her reddish blonde hair is matted, some of it torn out. The little face has a red rash from a few too many backhands. Mr. Howard instructed the CPS workers to get the truth out of her.

"I don't care how," Mr. Howard said. "All I know is that when I return I want to have in my hands the intimate details of her sexual experiences with her father, in script format."

And so it looks like the CPS workers beat the shit out of her, for goodness sake. One of the CPS workers tells me that they've been having a hard time with the interrogation.

"I can see that," I say, "but did you have to break her skin?"

Jill has a severe case of denial, she says. When she would ask a question regarding a nightmarishly incestuous relationship with her father, Jill would reply: "I love my Daddy. I want my Daddy." Apparently, she's been going on in this vein for hours.

Talk about sabotaging my cause.

The back-wall television flashes on. I push the buttons for Mr. Howard's Reality TV show to see if Mr. Howard is still at the crime scene with Meme's grandparents.

It looks like he has given the position of News Reporter to a CPS worker who watches over the two old people, Grandma and Grandpa Lamb, wire-strapped to a couple of chairs in the living room, surrounded by tripods with automatic zoom.

I approach Jill. Her face sulks downward, staring at the fingers she fidgets in each hand. I ask her to look up at me, but she doesn't move.

"Whoo-hoo!" I hear Mr. Howard howling from the back of the hall. "Whoo-hoo!"

Mr. Howard's vast figure skips down the red carpeted aisle, his mustache curved upward like two black bull horns. Pinhead and Stump clank the film equipment, following behind Mr. Howard as he works his way up the stairs to the stage.

"We have a problem," I say, pointing at Jill.

"What?" Mr. Howard asks, pouting his mustache. "Look at that sad little face! You can't help but feel sorry for her! We'll have the nation weeping on its knees!"

"She won't admit that she was molested," I say. "She's denying it. She wants to go home! Do you realize what this means?"

"It means you're going to have to work a little harder," Mr. Howard says. "I want that girl whining with the zeal of a radical feminist at a women's speak out contest! And I want to hear her anguished sob story by the end of the hour! We can't wait much longer! I've already advertised a full disclosure to appear on television! The entire world is standing by! They're waiting to see the little elfin Lamb girl all choked up and weeping on the television screen, speaking indiscriminately about the most private and embarrassing of sexual encounters with her father! And you're telling me that all you got is this *Leave it to Beaver* material? I don't think so."

He strokes his mustache and wobbles his large body over to Pinhead and directs him into position for the desired angle. Pinhead attaches a lens to the camera masking his face, adjusts the focus, and steps forward toward Jill. A CPS worker unfolds the ladder and places the spotlight on its swivel for Stump. Jill gasps in front of Pinhead's camera, flinches her face when Stump spotlights her eyes.

I ask a CPS worker to bring me the anatomically correct doll of the male gender and a bottle of amytal. I usually don't have to go this far. A child usually picks up on the signs, says what I want to hear, and the case is closed in a matter of minutes.

A commotion breaks out in the back of the theater. Three CPS stooges stumble toward the stage, the leader of the pack holding a portable phone in her hand.

"Carol," the CPS worker says, tramping up the steps, "there's a girl on the phone. She says she needs your help. She's been calling the Abuse Hotline all morning long. Her father is molesting her. He's raping her..."

"I can't believe this," Mr. Howard says. "It's moments like this that make me question everything. While I'm trying to make history, you clowns are haranguing Carol with the details of an obscene phone call! Are you deaf and blind, as well as dumb? Can't you see that Carol is busy trying to do her job? Somebody's got to do some work around here! You should take a break from the fun and games and give her a hand! That I've made it this far, with a comedy troupe, is itself a miracle! A testament to the supremacy of my vision!"

"It's a little girl!" the CPS worker says. "An incest victim!"

"Tell her to call the police," Mr. Howard says.

"She already called them...last week," the CPS worker says. "But they're tied up with the show..."

"Look," Mr. Howard says, "Carol can't be everywhere at once! She's trying to help *this* girl!"

Mr. Howard points Jill out for them, to whom they direct their dull faces.

"But she..."

"Give me the phone," Mr. Howard and I say at the same time.

"No," Mr. Howard says, "give *me* the phone."

"Give me the phone!" I say.

The stooge fumbles the phone into my hand.

"Hello," I say, pressing the phone against my face, "to whom am I speaking?"

"April Laurels," the girl says softly.

"April," I say, "this is not a good time. Can I get your number? Your address? I'll have somebody check in on you…"

"I'm being molested by my father," she cries quietly. "Why won't anybody help me? He's sexually abusing me. I don't have anyplace to go."

The girl cries so loud I have to hold the phone away from my ear. Mr. Howard walks toward me and reaches his fat hand out to grab the phone, but I won't let him. I turn and walk away; he follows me across the stage.

"Where is your mother?" I ask. "Is she home?"

"I don't know," the girl says. "She left. A month ago."

"Please hold on," I say.

I cover the phone with my palm.

"She's really being abused," I say.

"Sure," Mr. Howard says. "Of course. Her and everybody else who wants to be a star! We don't have all day."

He takes a swipe at the phone, but his hands are too thick and clumsy to take it from me.

"Don't," I say. "Why don't we do something? Put her on the show if we have to. She's got to be better than that wallflower over there."

I gesture toward Jill—still sitting in her chair like a deaf mute. I put the phone to my ear again.

"April," I say. "April, are you still there?"

"Yes," she says.

"April," I say, "tell me…"

Mr. Howard grabs my wrist and squeezes so tightly it feels like he's breaking it. I lose my grip on the phone and he takes it away from me. I hear him say:

"April, I'm sorry, but auditions are closed. In fact, we're thinking about letting some of the women go. Please forgive me for being so abrupt, but we have a lot of important work to do. We'll send some flowers later. Take care."

Mr. Howard peers over Pinhead's shoulder, slowly pushing him in for a close-up of Jill. I lift the anatomically correct doll from my desk and hold it in front of her.

"Look at what I've got here," I say, handing her the anatomically correct doll. Jill wraps both her arms around the doll. I open the bottle of amytal and hold it to her lips. "This will make you feel a lot better."

Jill's mouth cracks open and she drinks the fluid down. She looks back up at me through her swollen eyelids and cries little clear tears. She lifts a tiny hand up to her mouth and lightly taps her split lip; she wipes the amytal off her chin.

"We have a lot to talk about, don't we?"

Jill looks down at the doll strangled in her bruised arms.

"I...don't...know," she says.

I don't know. My entire life is on the line and you don't know? Could this possibly be any worse? Everything depends on one very simple thing: That you know!

"There is a little voice in my head telling me some things have happened," I say. "Do you want to talk about it?"

Jill sits there quietly, twitching her lips. She moves the doll to one arm and places the free hand on a swollen black eye.

"Jill," I say, "did your daddy do bad things to you?"

I'm paying close attention to her facial expression and whether or not she finds this discussion awkward. Any clues, little openings that I can pry open. Jill looks at me as though she doesn't know what I'm talking about. I hope this is shyness.

"I have a feeling that something happened to you," I say. "Don't you remember being abused in bizarre ways by your parents? Did your parents hang you from hooks in the basement?"

She squeezes the doll into her chest. Mr. Howard rubs his hands together. He could conquer the entire country in less than five seconds with a prepubescent girl crying on Reality TV about the loss of her virginity to her father.

"Jill," I say, "I'm trying to help you. I'm your friend. I know this must be hard for you. But if you just do as I say then everything will turn out right. You have to trust me."

"I want to go home," Jill pouts, looking down at her lap.

"If you want to see your mom and dad again," I say, "you need to tell me the truth. You need to admit that your daddy molested you."

Mr. Howard motions for me to sit in the chair next to Jill so that Pinhead can get us both on film. Pinhead backpedals out of a close-up, zooming his lens back into the camera. I lean down at Jill's side, kneeling on my knees. I softly caress her swollen cheek.

"Jill, do you want to see your mom again?" I ask her.

"Yes," Jill drops the doll into her lap, cups her face with her hands.

"If you don't tell me what your daddy did to you," I say, caressing her hand, "then you may never see your mom again."

"I love my mom and dad," Jill cries into her palms.

She wipes her little hands all over her face, then bows over.

"Everything is going to be okay," I say.

Jill forces her eyes open to look up at me as I pull up a chair and sit next to her. I take the doll from her lap and hold it up to her face.

"Look at that!" I say in my baby-talk voice, flicking my finger on the doll's little penis. "Do you know what that is? It's kind of funny looking, isn't it? Have you ever seen one before?" Jill looks away from me and into the lens of Pinhead's camera. I hold the stuffed doll closer to her face. "What is it?"

Jill just sits there, dumbfounded.

"Touch it," I say, "it won't bite you."

I try to guide Jill's tiny hand over the stuffed genitalia, but she won't go anywhere near it.

"Is that what daddy made you do?" I ask her.

"I want uh guh hum," Jill blubbers.

The medication is kicking in: her eyes are glossing over; the dulled reflexes, the upturned arms and limp wrists, the slack-jaw and drool. With the pharmaceutical industry, my job gets easier and easier. Sooner or later, it's going to put me out of work.

"Led me guh hum," Jill says. "I wanna guh hum…"

"Jill," I say, "I told you. All you have to do is open up to me and tell me what happened. Just answer my questions correctly and you can do whatever you want, I promise. Just tell the truth."

Jill looks like a lifeless porcelain doll, hanging her head down, mumbling vowel sounds.

"I…eee…ooo," she says, blowing invisible bubbles.

Mr. Howard paces back and forth behind Pinhead. He hasn't lit up a cigar since he's been here.

Jill's head swivels loosely on her neck as Pinhead pans a full circle. I hear Mr. Howard stomp across the stage; he is exiting with his briefcase in his hand. My job isn't so difficult that he couldn't replace me in less than five minutes. He could put any name on those self-help books and they would still sell like beanie babies.

"Just say 'Yes' to your mother and father," I whisper.

Jill finally lifts her face and stares at me through her watery blue eyes. She coughs out a mouthful of saliva, gaping in the direction of Stump's spotlight.

The stage is eerily silent for a few seconds, not even a whimper. Mr. Howard stops at the edge of the stage with his back turned on me, then he takes another step. Pinhead's camera zooms in on a glistening tear that falls across Jill's cheek. I reach over and with both hands pick Jill up by the front of her dress.

"If you don't start talking, Jill, you'll never see your family again. Your mother and father will spend the rest of their lives in prison. And you'll spend your little life camping out in at least a hundred foster homes before you reach the age of sixteen. I'm giving you one more chance to save yourself and your helpless parents. Tell me what I want to hear. Tell me that you were molested by your father. I don't *care* if it's real!"

Jill kicks her feet into my stomach and the fabric of her dress begins to stretch, rips. My hand catches on her hair, pulling strands out of her head. Jill's cry comes to a sudden end with a hollow thump as her head hits the stage floor. Her neck is twisted unnaturally off to one side. I don't see any blood.

A long, ominous silence fills the auditorium, followed by an asthmatic rattle as Mr. Howard inhales.

"Whoo-hoo!" Mr. Howard howls. He lights a cigar. "Whoo-hoo!"

I can't even speak. I move the chair away from Jill and kneel down, pushing into her chest. It's like poking a dead animal with a stick.

"Whoo-hoo!" Mr. Howard puffs white smoke out of his mouth. "Pinhead, I want you to pan a full circle and then spiral in for a close-up."

Stump's spotlight shines brightly into my eyes.

"Come on, Jill," I pull her body. "Get up! Wake up!"

I hold her mouth open and bend over. I put my lips on her lips, blowing air into her mouth. Her cheeks expand and expel the air back out. Pinhead's camera hums above my head.

"Call an ambulance!" I scream out.

Mr. Howard doesn't move, and neither does anyone else.

"Call an ambulance!"

"Carol," Mr. Howard says, "you need to calm down. Get ahold of yourself."

"Oh God!" I say. "We need a doctor!"

"Get her some Valium," Mr. Howard says.

"Why are you just standing there? Somebody do something!"

An assistant gives me some pills and some water. Mr. Howard walks over and pulls me up off the floor. He places his huge hands on my shoulders and shakes me violently.

"You need to stop this right now," Mr. Howard says. "Control yourself. We'll call the police and tell them that she tripped and fell. You are a healer. You help people. You have nothing to worry about. The world thinks you are an angel! I will take care of everything. Stop acting hysterical."

Mr. Howard hands me the portable phone. He tells me what to say. She tripped and fell.

The medical report was terrible, but not the end of the world. Jill suffered a concussion and a neck injury. The doctor said she'd be out for a month. Mr. Howard says it's a good thing. It was the best thing that could have happened. Jill was a liability. He told me to think in terms of natural selection. The elimination of the unfit. Jill proved to be ill-adapted for the environment of his theater and the proper evolution of a public hysteria.

"You can't blame Darwin or yourself for that," Mr. Howard said.

I asked, "What about the film footage?"

"That's taken care of," Mr. Howard said. "I burned the reel of film. It's a pile of ash and carnage."

But I have my doubts. Especially after he tells me that my share of the profits are being wiped out.

Chapter 11
▼

THROW IT AGAINST THE WALL AND SEE WHAT STICKS

Little Barbie dolls lay all over the hardwood floors. A play-house is flattened and scattered in one corner of the apartment. Matchbox cars and marbles move about the floor as I walk out of the bathroom. I have to slide my slippers across the floor to get to where I'm going. I'm half asleep, rubbing my eyes; when I look up, I see Meme wearing nothing but an over-sized diaper, sucking on her thumb.

"Googygoo," she says.

"What?"

"Googah," she says.

"This is just great," I say.

I haven't had breakfast and the day is already ruined. Meme pulls her thumb out of her mouth and smiles. She bounces on her ass, causing her breasts to bob up and down.

"I see," I say. "You are a prepubescent child. I am a pedophile. And I'm supposed to molest you?"

"Gahgah," she says.

I'm not sure if that's a yes. I walk over to the couch and sit down. The big sex abuse book is opened up on the coffee table. A couple sentences get my attention:

"Let yourself be a baby for a day. Have the kind of childhood you always wanted!"

"Googygahgahgoo," Meme sounds out.

"Is this supposed to help you," I ask, pointing at her diaper, "take control of your childhood?"

Meme inserts her thumb into her mouth and smiles.

"Ahgah," Meme says.

I notice some wooden alphabet blocks on the floor where Meme has spelled: POOP.

"I see," I say. "Meme, there must be a more sophisticated way to overcome the trauma, the trauma of your *self*."

She picks up a doll and brushes its hair. Horrible sounds come from the area of her diaper, producing an invisible, asphyxiating cloud. I have to move to the other side of the room. She cries into her chest for a while and then stretches her arms out to me, dropping the doll and comb to the floor. Shit squirts out of her diaper like thick, dark mustard. Meme points at me, then at her diaper; I realize, almost immediately, what she is trying to tell me, what she wants me to do.

"I'm not changing your diaper," I say.

I pace around the apartment, holding my hands to my face, to my nose. I grab the trash can from the kitchen and come back and frantically stuff dolls and hairbrushes and play-house kits into the can, stomping it down with my foot.

I return to the kitchen for some large Glad Bags.

"Stop it!" Meme cries out—not in baby-talk, I notice—and starts thrashing her body on the floor.

She reaches down and tears the diaper off. Drippy shit flings across the hardwoods.

"Meme, don't, please," I say, staring while she whips the brownish-yellow diaper through the air.

I duck up and down, dodging the spray of shit as if it were bullets.

"Kaka! Kaka! Kaka!"

"Meme," I say, "please…this is my home…"

"Kaka!"

She throws the diaper against the wall where it smacks loudly and sticks.

"Oh," I moan.

Meme points at the diaper on the wall, then smacks her palms on her thighs and giggles at the shit-stained room. She says, softly now, "Kaka. Kaka. Kaka."

The Glad Bag drops from my hand. The flies are back for a feast, doing circles around the center of the studio. Meme claps her shit-painted hands.

I find a clean corner of the couch and sit down and light a cigarette while Meme finger-paints with her feces on the floor: a smaller stick figure gives a bigger stick figure head. I stare up at the ceiling.

"I can't take this anymore." I inhale a long drag. "I am going to kill you!"

Meme lifts her head toward me, and with her fingers she draws lines beneath her eyes. She looks like an Amazon warrior.

"You think I'm dirty," Meme says, "because I was raped and molested."

Standing in the aisle where diapers are stocked in large puffy bags. The book said for a day, but I buy the economy size to play it safe. Twelve Huggies in all. I also grab some baby food. Mashed carrots. Mashed bananas. And some chocolate pudding.

When I return, I see that Meme has taken the crayons to the walls. She claps gleefully when I arrive with diapers, and more ecstatically after I help her tie one on. She crawls around the apartment, gahgahing, chewing on crayons. Her face and lips—blue, green, red. She tries to eat the bottom of a high-heel, and I don't try to stop her.

In the kitchen, I crack open Meme's Sex Victim Kit and dig through the orange pill containers in search of sedatives and muscle relaxants. I smash and grind and blend Valium, Restoril, and Halcion into a fine powder, stir the pill concoction into a jar of mashed bananas. I approach Meme with the spiked baby food. I put on a big smile and hold the little jar of Gerber in front of her. She swings her arm at me and knocks it on the floor.

She crawls over to the Yellow Pages, finds the page she's looking for, and jabs her finger for me to come see.

She's pointing at the advertisement for Foucault's, one of the finer, more romantic, French restaurants in town.

"No," I say. "We are not going out in public. I'm not taking you out like this."

The maitre d' is nervous. There is a dress code, he says.

Foucault's is on the top floor of the tallest building in the city and is very crowded tonight. Two jazz musicians lightly strum a bass and brush a drum in a corner of the candlelit restaurant. The city view glows with the reflection of the moon on river and night lights like still lanterns. Cars string across bridges like fluorescent yellow bulbs. And Meme will have a table near the window or the elegant ambiance of Foucault's will turn into a sewer of muck and disorder.

"Dear Sir," I say, "this is a fragment of *la femme fatale*, Meme Lamb. The Greatest Victim of All Time! Disciple of that Dishonorable Circe, Carol Porter, Princess of Humbugs and Revolutionary of Innards. I'm sure you have heard of her."

I put my arm around *l'enfant terrible*. Meme's face is still colored in rainbow colors of crayon wax. Two large safety pins hold the white diaper up to her hips. Her breasts poke upward and unshaved arm pit and body hair vines its way over her skin.

"Now this may all mean absolutely nothing to you," I say, grimacing, "but I will accept no responsibility whatsoever for the apocalyptic consequences that will surely follow if you should decide to say no to this," pause, "...Lady." Meme's eyes are watering, the wax is melting, and the flicker of a cry begins. "Dear Sir, if Meme does not get what she wants, you will know the wrath of her scorn!"

"Look!" a woman says, unwrapping a bandage from her wrist while she pushes into Meme. "I'm a victim too!"

Meme signs an autograph with a crayon on a cloth napkin. The woman runs back to her table.

Insulted and offended and whatever, the couple sitting at the table that is to become Meme's scurry out of the restaurant in a cantankerous manner. Other patrons whisper and stare, smile and wave. Most of them politely leave with their dinners half-finished on their plates, walking out with cloth napkins covering their faces. A few die-hard Meme fans and what's left of a company party remain. Meme googahs while a waitress ties a bib around her neck.

"Sorry," the waitress makes a cute little baby face at Meme, "we don't have a high-chair big enough."

Meme orders just about everything. Dungeness crab cakes. Duck with blackberry sauce. Grilled venison with a sun-dried cherry vinaigrette. Other dishes I cannot pronounce.

I order a bottle of port. Two bottles of wine. Several straight shots without ice. I stir up a cocktail of sorts in a clear milk bottle with a rubber nipple and add a couple of Valium to the mix. The combination of alcohol and psychiatric drugs should knock Meme to the ground, just long enough for me to get a good night's sleep, maybe figure things out.

But Meme doesn't drink anything. She paints the table with her dinner and sends waitresses hurdling in the air to catch a slab of lamb or a crab cake headed toward one of the few remaining patrons. She tries to put in another order when there's no more food left to throw. The chef comes out, screaming furiously: "The kitchen is closed!"

When we get back to my apartment, I try to talk Meme into changing her diaper. I'm being as gentle as possible to prevent a tantrum, but she won't listen. She sits down on the red velvet couch; the diaper squishes and burbles. More shit leaks out. She hunches over *The Malleus Porculorum* and turns the page to read about the next step on the road to recovery.

And she's only half-way through the book.

At midnight, we are playing charades. She changes personalities and I guess her name.

I meet Cinderella, who against all odds manages to rise above the cruel circumstances of destitution and hardship to become famous and cherished by all. We do a little ballroom dance.

I meet Rodney King during his historic moment. Meme wails and throes and is nearly bludgeoned to death in the corner of my apartment near her Gucci bag filled with shoes from Saks Fifth Avenue.

I meet Chief Joseph after his last battle. Meme mourns the death of the coffee table, the rug, the TV and her mink coat as if they are dead Nez Perce warriors.

And then my luck begins to change. Meme puts on a red miniskirt and a skimpy bra, a string of pearls and white high heels, feathers her hair with some hairspray, à la Farrah Fawcett. Her name is Natalia, she says, a woman who escaped the ruins of the Soviet Union. Claims to have crossed the ocean as a sex slave on the black market. She wants to know something.

"Are you my customer?"

I say: "Yes."

"Where's the money?"

I pull out a wad of cash. She counts it and says:

"Twenty-three dollars?"

"It's all I have."

"Do I get to keep all of it?"

I explain to her that we need to go someplace else. A parking lot. A hotel room. We can't be here in the event that my girlfriend comes home.

"It could get ugly," I say.

She agrees.

Outside, I direct Natalia toward Meme's white Volvo. She staggers at the pace of a snail, tripping every few steps over the high heels. She finally gets in the car and we drive down the street.

"There is so much variety," she says, pointing her finger at a restaurant. "That soup kitchen looks so elegant!"

"That's a restaurant," I say.

"They must have very good soup," she says.

It is as if Meme has undergone a physical metamorphosis. Natalia's features are more defined, seductively striking.

Natalia talks and talks. Hangs her head out the window of the Volvo; her silky, red hair flies in the wind. She feels so free, she says, laughing.

"Compared to the Soviet Union," Natalia says, while we cruise under the moon shadows of tall fir trees and wind on the narrow road to the coast, "America is paradise."

And the people are so sweet to her, she says. They always pay top-rate.

"Where are we going?" she asks. "This is a long drive."

"We're going to the coast," I say. "I have a house on the beach."

"Really?" she asks. "I can't wait to see it."

It belongs to Meme's parents, but I can't really say that.

And I can't take my eyes off her. She is so beautiful. The way she laughs, the way she strokes her neck with her hand. The way she licks her lips. My mind fills up with fantasies of the kinkiest kind.

I turn off onto a cobblestone road and approach a large iron gate. I push the buttons on a controller; the gates open and close behind. Natalia hops out of the Volvo. As she runs off, the red miniskirt rides up above two sweetly round cheeks.

The beach house is three levels high and set on the edge of a cliff. I use Meme's keys to open the back door while Natalia stands in front looking out at the wild blue ocean. I search throughout the house, all three levels, for photographs of Meme and her family and stash them in a closet. I kind of mess it up a little, make it look like a bachelor's pad. I unplug the phone, just in case.

I walk out the front door, through tall white Roman columns, and stand beside her. Natalia takes my hand and I follow her down the dirt path to the beach. She prances around in the cold water and unsnaps the white chiffon bra and drops it into the sea. Funny, I think to myself, since Meme has a fear of water. Her pearl necklace slinks softly against her nipples. She walks back up to the sand and wraps her arms around me. She unbuttons my shirt, takes off my shoes, unzips my pants and pulls them down with my underwear to my ankles.

She lays down and sprawls on the white sand, pulling me on top of her, gently caressing my cock. She presses me against her, rapidly kisses my face; sucks on my neck, my ear. She slides up over me and wraps my mouth around a nipple; it flares within my mouth. I slowly move my hand down to her vagina. Her legs flex around my waist.

I'm so horny, everything about Natalia is sweet, voluptuous, something to eat. The slits on her wrists look like chocolate covered rosebuds. The bruises that pattern her body taste like raspberries. The dead, medicated, blood-shot eyes look like wine. I could drink from them forever.

She holds the base of my cock while I penetrate her, then lets it go wild. I thrust feverishly, desperately, like it has been years and years. Natalia's body vibrates and howls, cranks and moans. I've got rhythm, a harmonious motion, until I hear a thousand voices shrieking from Meme's body.

This is no orgasm, I despair. It's like watching a woman give birth in an *Alien* sequel. I hear a revolver sound, a chattering of teeth, and a wheel spinning round and round inside her head. I'm losing momentum. My cock is becoming a limp rubberband.

I pull it out just as she asks:

"What are you doing? Why are we naked? What are you doing between my legs?"

"Nothing," I say. "Nothing."

Meme reaches for her seaweed soaked miniskirt, and her purse, which she empties out onto the sand. She's looking for something. Her lipstick? The white powder? She's flinging dollar bills into the air—the money that I paid her. I jump to my feet and hold my hands in front of me. I try to explain:

"I was just…I was just," I stammer.

"Trying to rape me?"

"Meme, please."

"Trying to rape one of my alters?"

"She was a hooker," I say, holding up several dollars. "I paid her. I paid her."

Meme flies through the air and lands on top of me. I feel her hand wrap around my penis. In her other hand, something clicks. A switchblade. I push myself away and fall on my back in the sand. I roll away and crawl on all fours toward the water. Meme never learned how to swim.

"I'm going to wait," she says. "I've got all night." She curls her lip, fiercely clicks the switchblade in and out. "And when you fall asleep, while you are dreaming peacefully, I'm going to cut your cock off and throw it in a ditch."

She laughs.

I continue to wade, treading my feet and legs. There, on the shore, Meme waits. A few more minutes and I'll probably drown. She stands there and stares, chewing on pills to calm herself down.

Meme finally drops to her knees and falls face forward into the sand. I swim back to shore; trembling, I put my shirt and pants on. I check her pulse. She's breathing. I loosen the switchblade from her grip and toss it out into the ocean.

"Meme," I say. "Meme."

I turn her over so that she's on her back. I slap her in the face, but she's out cold.

I make sure the rope is tightly secured to the chair. I want her to be restrained when she finally wakes in the throes of withdrawal. The withdrawal of self-addiction. No more self-help books. No more self-medicating. No more staring into mirrors.

I find a bottle of Scotch. I sniff the fumes and take a swig. Meme smacks her cotton mouth; I wet mine with another sip.

"Frank," I hear Natalia whisper.

"Yes," I say.

"Frank," Natalia says, "why are you doing this to me?"

I stare deeply and closely into Natalia's eyes, in search of a different species.

"Because you are not really there," I say. "You are not really there."

I look out the window, at its panoramic view. The sun rests beautifully on the horizon, like a Kitsch painting you might buy on the highway. And the strangest thing happens. The curtains close on their own.

[Intermission]

Two stagehands walk into the living room. Frank looks over at them with little interest. He sits very calm and still. He swigs the bottle of whisky. One stagehand rolls the dining room table off the stage. The other stagehand picks up a lamp from a nightstand, then walks away. Bill Howard appears, wearing a white tuxedo and holding a cane. He instructs a stagehand to break down the bay window. Frank takes another drink.

FRANK: I want to go home.

BILL HOWARD: Somebody get him backstage.

A stagehand walks over and tries to lift Frank from the chair.

STAGEHAND: He's drunk. I'm going to need some help over here.

BILL HOWARD: No, those whisky bottles are filled with water. See if Stewart's still got his doctor's uniform. We need to have him looked at. Have him checked for pneumonia.

Another stagehand approaches Frank from behind. The two stagehands wrap Frank's arms over their shoulders and heave him out of the chair, the whisky bottle still clutched in his hand. They haul Frank toward the back of the stage. Mr. Howard unties Meme's arms and legs.

MEME: What happened to the show? Did I miss the show?

BILL HOWARD: Meme, you were absolutely wonderful! You were masterful! But it's not over. The best part is yet to come. *He helps Meme up from the chair.* Somebody put a blanket around her. *A stagehand wraps her in a beach towel.* Take her back to the dressing room and get her cleaned up.

Mr. Howard instructs a stagehand to drain the pool and vacuum the sand.

Chapter 12

▼

THE MANSION OF SALVATION

Today's turnout is about as expected. I only had four remaining survivors of the original support group. There were a few predictable suicides. Cassandra finally overdosed. And Mr. Howard felt that it was necessary to cut some clients from the team. After eight weeks, Betty only managed to come up with two personalities. Sally, who at first appeared to be an MPD protégé, weaned and maxed out at thirteen. And then there is Michelle, who survived the first round of the team cut, but not the second. Her insurance ran out.

"Michelle Agatha," I call out. "I need to talk to you, there seems to be a problem, some bad news."

Michelle Agatha stops at stage-right.

"What?" Michelle asks. "What's wrong?"

I put my arm around her shoulder and walk with her across the stage to the stairs.

"I need to speak to you in private," I say.

We walk down the steps and up the red carpeted aisle to the lounge area. We stop in front of the stainless steel popcorn machine. The yellow popcorn glows through the front glass. The smell of salted butter is thick in the air. I ask the CPS worker behind the counter to give us two medium-sized bags of popcorn and a couple of sodas.

"Michelle," I say. "Michelle, it looks like your insurance coverage has run out. It will no longer pay for the support groups or therapy sessions."

I pat her on the back. We are both standing there staring into the stainless steel siding of the popcorn machine. It reflects a surreal image of the two of us, two people staring into warped mirrors, warped images of ourselves.

"And that means," I cough, "you are no longer a part of the team."

Michelle slowly hyperventilates, then digs her chewed up fingernails into her temples. Dry heaves for several minutes. The CPS worker hands me the bags of popcorn. I try to give one to Michelle.

"No," she whispers.

I watch her wrap her arms around herself, hugs and hugs, dipping her head down and up and down again with tears.

"No...no...no...no...Carol...I...beg...you...please..."

She reaches out to me. Her thin arms wave in front of her like two shot electrical wires.

"There's nothing I can do."

I take a bite of the fresh, warm, buttery popcorn.

"I'll pay cash." She says, crying, "I'll do anything. You are all I have."

Her mouth sounds like a typewriter on speed while she removes the rest of her fingernails with her already ground-down teeth. She falls to the floor near my feet.

"I'll get a job," she says, hugging my ankles.

I'm kicking my feet and tap-dancing while I try to get her face off my shoes.

"How are you going to get a job?" I ask. "Who is going to hire a thirty-two-year-old anorexic who weighs eighty pounds and has fifteen personalities?"

The CPS worker sets the sodas on the countertop.

"Carol...what...can...I...do?" Her face breaks out in hives. "Where can I go?"

"Go...home," I say, reaching for a soda to wash the popcorn down.

Michelle kicks and switches in and out of multiple personalities.

"But...I," she says, moaning, "sold my home," she gags, "to pay my medical bills."

She burps out acid from her empty stomach. I offer her some soda but she refuses. I tell her that I hate to let her go. That it makes me sad. That we have a relationship that actually matters. But the truth is, I hardly know her. The only things I really know about Michelle are the things that I've told her about herself. Things that I knew before I even met her. She came to me one day not so long ago because she was having bad dreams. Nightmares that made her think that something awful was going to happen to her.

I instruct several CPS workers to drag Michelle out of the theater.

My CPS workers already have Meme knocked out and shaking from a high dose of amytal when I return to the stage. She's set for another hypnotherapy session.

I lift both of Meme's arms and acknowledge the sliced up wrists. I tell her that she needs to stop doing that. Mr. Howard has instructed me to get Meme to stop the self-mutilation therapy. She's our main attraction; if we lose her, we lose the show.

"Because you let the elfin Lamb girl go," he grumbled.

I review the Black List Mr. Howard prepared for me. He says that he wants the accusations to reach into the national arena: politicians, athletes, rock stars. He even selected a few names from the afterlife, among those the famous scientist, Carl Sagan. Sagan once publicly dismissed claims that aliens are abducting people and molesting them.

I'm talking to Meme about her childhood, the Satanic ritual abuse, and what it was like to grow up in The Cult.

"Do you remember the coven?" I ask.

"The coven?"

"There is something on the altar. Isn't there?"

"Yes," she cries.

"Are they about to sacrifice an animal?" I ask.

"Yes," Meme says, wiping tears out of her eyes, "my poodle."

"They ate him," I say, "didn't they?"

"Yes…yes…they…they…ate him," she says.

"Who?" I sit up straight. "Who? Was Carl Sagan in on it?"

I show Meme a photograph of Carl Sagan. It's a cut and paste job of a man wearing a black robe. He's breaking a rabbit's neck and letting the blood pour into a basin.

"Was it this person?" I ask. "Carl Sagan?"

"Yes," she says, "Carol Saga. Yes. Carol Saga was in it."

"No," I say, "Carl! Car…L. Sagan. S. A. G. A. N."

She cries, tears roll down her face, more shaking.

"Yes…yes," Meme says. "Carol Satan was in on it, too. With Carol Saigon."

"No," I say. "Carl! Sagan!"

Meme mumbles.

"Remember Carl Sagan raping you?" I ask. "Molesting you? He's a Satanic pedophile isn't he?"

"I hate Carol," Meme says. "I was raped by Carol Saga."

"Carl...Carl...Carl," I say. "Carl Sagan slit Ralph's throat and poured poodle's blood all over you! Carl Sagan forced you to eat dead human flesh, didn't he?"

"Yes," Meme spits out an invisible chunk of meat. "Carol Satan made me eat the sacrifice victims."

"This isn't working," I tell Mr. Howard.

"I hate Carol Saigon," Meme says.

"Think extra-galactic breeder! Helen of the Stars!" Mr. Howard says through a speaker. "Think Pope mistress! Tales of drag and foot fetishes!"

I ask one of my assistants to bring me the E.T. doll and a rosary.

"Carol," a CPS worker says, "an investigator is outside. He wants to talk to you. He wants to know if you can see him right now?"

"Do...you know...what he wants?" I ask.

"Something to do with the Lamb family," she says.

"Tell him that we're in the middle of trial rehearsal," I say. "He'll have to come back tomorrow."

"He's coming in," a CPS worker yells out from the back of the auditorium. "He said he has to meet you right away. He's in the lobby."

Mr. Howard howls out for everyone to take five.

"Get her backstage," I point at Meme.

"Carol is a pedophile," Meme slurs while the CPS worker pushes the wheeled chaise longue to the side of the stage and through an exit.

A man comes walking slowly down the red aisle and steps cautiously up to the stage. He greets me with a kind smile.

"Hello, I'm Carol," I tell him.

"Nice to meet you," he says. "My name is Joe Morris. I'm an investigator working on the Lamb case."

"Please sit down."

Joe Morris looks, from up close, like he's probably in his fifties. He has a slightly bald white head. A dark blue business suit stretches around his thick limbs. He sits down in the chair opposite my desk.

"I've heard a lot of good things about you," he says.

I give him the affirmation of a smile.

"How long have you been a therapist?"

"A couple of years."

Joe Morris writes some notes down on his white pocket-tablet.

"I just want to ask you some questions," he says, "some questions regarding the little girl. The one that ended up in the hospital?"

"Jill," I say.

"Yes, Jill," he says.

"We are all very shaken by the whole thing," I say. "We had no idea that her condition was that severe, that she was suffering from injuries, otherwise we would have had her treated immediately after removing her from her family."

"Yes," Joe Morris says, noting the pad again. "I understand. Now the other daughter, Meme. Is she doing okay?"

"Surprisingly," I say. "The emotional and physical abuse has had a severe effect. She is in therapy to help overcome the trauma. She's showing a great deal of promise. Of course, the healing process will take some time. But I'd say her rate of recovery so far is unheard of. All she really needs is a little attention."

"I sincerely hope for the best," Joe Morris says. He pulls out a picture and shows it to me. "Are you familiar with this girl?"

I look at the picture: a girl's body—a rope tightly noosed around a head of hair at one end and tied to the thick branch of a tree at the other.

"It's kind of hard to tell," I say. "You can't really see her face."

"Her name is April Laurels," he says. "Thought maybe you might know of her. She hung herself this morning from a tree in the backyard of her house. Her father had been molesting her, according to the suicide note. She said that she tried to seek help. I just thought that might mean something to you."

I lapse into a trance.

In a nightmare I had last night, the stage in the Paris Theater looked like an emergency room filled with unaided car crash victims, a junkyard of weathered mannequins, a bombed M.A.S.H. unit stocked with burned limbs and faces melting into the elements. Soaked in blood, hundreds of dead bodies lay in a heap on the stage floor like dead Jews on a Nazi concentration camp wagon. Little girls, little boys. Men and women. Some bodies were torn apart so badly I couldn't identify age or gender. I tried to lift some of the bodies but their heads, arms, and legs snapped off when I pulled them. My knees were soaked with blood and my arms were a dark red all the way up to my elbows. Sheets of human skin stuck to my arms like wet autumn leaves. Some of the older corpses were laminated to the floor. A constant wailing echoed throughout the auditorium, the acoustics of the dead were sharp and clear. I was digging through the pile, getting warmer and deeper, breathing in the smell of death all around me.

There was a corpse-statue of Mrs. Lamb with her cheeks eroded, arms extended, yearning for her daughter who leaned toward her less than three feet away like a breathing Ethiopian skeleton. Jill was whispering, "I want to go home."

Carcasses were in piles across the stage, clients divorced from their ruined lives. Innocent youth protected from the insanity of modern times. Deadly families with their pieces scattered. Children I saved from torturous home lives. People who'd walked through the Gates of Help with a stupendous will to survive.

Black-framed photographs of other families who had experienced my therapeutic services hung on the back wall of the stage. The photographs were for sale and exhibited as cutting-edge postmodern art. In one corner was a box of anatomically correct dolls. In another area were boxes filled with gold fillings, jewelry, and expensive watches.

Families stood in a line that stretched down the red carpeted aisle, out of the theater, and around the block. They were all coming to me for help. These people who couldn't stand each other and their broken marriages. Parents wanting to put their children on medication. People with all the things they never wanted.

In my dream, all these people were coming to me and asking that I perform an impossible miracle. For this was where the sick brought their diseases. Where the empty came like blow-up dolls waiting to be stuffed with the meat of meaning. This was where the wounded came to mourn the death of their souls. The disillusioned. The sad. The cheated. The have-nots. The dreamers. And the self-defeated. The wannabe, fated to never be.

"Come!" Mr. Howard announced over the congregation. "Be blessed with the touch of Carol's New Age Balm of Gilead! Enter through the Gates of Help and she'll anesthetize your sorrows! She is a doctor! A healer! A miracle worker! She can turn your shame and self-loathing, your little life of big regrets, into a heroic semblance with a glorious bent!"

"Carol, are you okay?"

I look up and see a man standing in front of me.

"The girl in the picture," he says, "you've never heard of her?"

"No," I say, "I don't think so. We get so many phone calls. This is a busy time. We have so much work. It's impossible to keep up."

He takes the picture back and stares brokenheartedly at the image before tucking it back into his jacket pocket. He pauses for a few seconds and silently reads over his notes.

"I understand that you work with anatomically correct dolls."

I nod.

"Do you videotape your sessions?" he asks.

"Yes."

"Do you think I could take a look at the video of Jill's session?" Joe Morris asks. "I would like to review it just to acquaint myself with your therapeutic techniques."

My hands are trembling quite badly so I hide them under my desk. Mr. Morris widens his eyes and opens his mouth, but doesn't say anything. I shake my head no. I don't say anything.

"The video?" he says, "would it be alright if I had a look at the video?"

"Well," I say, "I don't know. The video? We lost the video. It got ruined. My assistant lost it. I think. You know," I clap my hands together, "I don't think we taped that session."

"You didn't videotape the session?" Joe Morris asks, "or you lost the tape?"

"Yes," I say. "We decided not to…"

"Or it was ruined?"

I'm tapping my fingers on the top of my desk, pretending to contemplate the issue.

"No," I say, "we decided to hold off on that one…"

"It was a very important session," Joe Morris says. "Why wouldn't you videotape the session?"

"She was…really shy," I say. "She didn't want to say anything. Stage fright. Something. The little girl was traumatized. We didn't want to put any more pressure on her than was necessary. It would have been a very depressing experience for everyone. You know what I mean?"

"Yes," he says.

I can feel a bead of sweat crawling down around my lip.

Joe Morris gets up out of the chair and paces across the stage floor. He stops at center stage. There is something about his eyes. A look not at all flattering or trying to flatter.

"Can you tell me some specifics about the Lamb family?" he asks.

I feel like I'm about to faint. The stage looks like it is warping, splintering the boards, turning them into arms. I see former clients and children laying on the hardwood floor. Their bodies are half-clothed and half-fleshed. They seem to be rooted into the stage, like living props designed for this Theater of Misery. Their mouths are making sad guppy faces, taking little bites out of the air. I look out at the audience and see Mothers and Fathers dressed in black and lined up and down the red carpeted aisle, waiting to step into my funeral parlor. To say their final goodbyes. To cry on my shoulder.

"Carol," Mr. Morris says, "can you tell me anything about the Lamb family?"

I can hardly get the words to come out of my mouth. The theater is silent. Joe Morris steps backward into the ocean of ghosts, their arms bent crooked in the air, slithering and writhing like eels. Their heads hang down their fronts and backs, faintly singing the harmony of the dead.

Joe Morris tilts his head down and sighs, staring at the floor. A ghost lifts her hand high enough to touch the area near his knee cap. Mr. Morris reaches down and scratches that part of his slacks.

"I saw the news clip of when you removed Jill from her home," Joe Morris says. "She seemed to be in fair condition at the time. No visible scars or physical damage from what I could gather. She appeared to be somewhat disoriented from all the excitement, but there was nothing I could see that suggests what was found in the medical report. Bone fractures and bruises up and down her arms and legs. Do you care to comment on that fact?"

He mistakes my nervous chill for a nod.

"When Jill left her home, her face wasn't black and blue," he says. "When she was delivered to the hospital after the visit to your office, she had abrasions across her forehead and broken ribs."

Arms twist like vines around Mr. Morris's ankles. I look up and pretend not to notice.

"She was so quiet about the abuse," I say. "In shock, I think. She wouldn't talk much. There were some minor bruises and scratches on her body. From a struggle with her parents. That's what she said; a beating from her father. When we brought her back here, she seemed fine, playing around like a girl. Then she tripped and fell."

"She tripped and fell?" Joe Morris asks.

"Just trying to be a kid again," I say, sadly.

Joe Morris folds up his white pocket-tablet and puts it in the inside pocket of his jacket. The arms and hands writhe and fall behind his shoe as he takes a step away from all of their pleas. He holds his hand over his mouth, as if trying to prevent himself from saying something.

"I should let you get back to work."

"Please let me know if I can do anything else for you," I say, rising out of my chair.

"I will, and you do the same," he says, handing me his business card. With a concerned face he adds, "If you come up with anything else, please give me a call."

"Yes...yes," I say, shaking his hand again, egging him off the stage.

The ghost of a dead girl drags herself with her arms as her legs flip after her like a fishtail. A snake track of blood winds its way behind her. Where her face should be, there is nothing. It's just a blur, a small black hole leading to nowhere.

Joe Morris stares at me, silent. I can feel my face blushed with sweat. He shakes off a chill running up his spine.

"I feel like I'm being touched by the ghost of that little girl," he says. "April Laurels. Like she's asking me to save her. To help her. To save the children."

Closing my eyes, I sigh, I nod.

When I open my eyes, the ghosts have disappeared. The stage is empty. There's nothing there anymore. Only the silence of the Theater of the Absurd.

I look at the business card. It reads:

Joe Morris
Actor
OSCAR'S TALENT AGENCY
We meet your theatrical needs!

CHAPTER 13
▼

BILL HOWARD'S REALITY TV LAW & ORDER

The Greatest Show on Earth
Season Finale
Script
by
Bill Howard

Standard courtroom setting. A large bronze State Seal is mounted on the back stage wall, above and behind the Judge who is ruling over the case; an American flag is to the left of the State Seal; a blown up photograph of April Laurels is to the right, placed as background to the panel. A jury sits in two rows on the far side, stage-right. Bill Howard is dressed in a white tux with a white hat on his head. He's wearing a black armband with gold-glitter lettering and trim; it says: April Laurels. Mr. Howard walks stage-right and places his briefcase on the plaintiff's table. He opens the briefcase and pulls out a microphone.

BILL HOWARD: Ladies and gentlemen! Welcome to "The Greatest Show on Earth." A special "Bill Howard's Reality TV Law & Order." We have an exciting show just for you! There will be more than one thousand guests on the stand today, most of them embodied in Meme Lamb. She is here today to give testimony of horrifying tales of sex abuse. We also have an expert on the show. Carol Porter is a specialist on Repressed Memory Syndrome, Multiple Personality Disorder, and the Road to Recovery. The Honorable Samuel Sewall will be presiding over today's events. Thank you once again, ladies and gentlemen, for stopping by and tuning in to "The Greatest Show on Earth: Bill Howard's Reality TV Law & Order." Welcome, welcome, welcome…

DEFENSE ATTORNEY: *Over loud cheers.* Your Honor, we haven't had enough time to prepare, we need more time. The defense begs you to allow…

BILL HOWARD: Objection, Your Honor, but you can hardly call that a defense! *He points his cane at Mr. Lamb.* Any extension would be a total waste of time and money. We have a packed house. Millions of people are tuned in for the show. We can't turn back now and postpone the trial. There will be a public outcry!

Mr. Howard approaches the judge's bench and shows him the Penile Plethysmograph test results.

JUDGE SEWALL: Three times?

Mr. Howard holds three fat fingers in front of Judge Sewall's face.

BILL HOWARD: Three times!

JUDGE SEWALL: Objection sustained! *He pounds his mallet on the desk.* Mr. Howard, please proceed.

The defense attorney walks slowly back to his table, staring at the ground. Mr. Howard tilts the flat white hat to one side on his head and leans on his white cane.

BILL HOWARD: Your Honor, I call Carol Porter to the stand.

Carol Porter is dressed in a black business suit and arm band. She walks onto the stage and steps up to the booth to the right of the judge. The audience gives a standing ovation. Over her shoulder, April Laurels hangs like an apparition in the wind, an ominous spirit lending authentication to the mood of Carol's funeral attire. Mr. Howard flips his white cane around his wrist and then jabs it into the stage floor.

BILL HOWARD: Carol, please tell the audience and the jury your name and your profession. And, if you will, explain to the court your relationship to Meme Lamb.

Carol looks down and reads from the script in her hands.

CAROL PORTER: My name is Carol Porter, of course, and I work as a therapist. I meet with Meme daily for private therapy sessions or in support group. I've been trying to help her recover from sexual abuse, so we try to meet as often as possible.

BILL HOWARD: Carol, you specialize in repressed memories. Will you please explain what that means.

CAROL PORTER: A client represses a memory of an experience when that experience is traumatic. It is a survival tactic.

BILL HOWARD: Was it obvious? *He holds the microphone to his mustache.* Could you recognize, right away, that your client, Meme, had a very unique and extraordinary background? How could you tell that Meme had been raped by her father all these years?

CAROL PORTER: It was obvious. Though I wouldn't say unique. This kind of thing happens every second, it is everywhere. Extraordinary, yes. It is truly outrageous that this happens and so few women stand up and talk about it.

BILL HOWARD: What was it? How could you tell?

CAROL PORTER: Meme clearly demonstrated signs of post-traumatic stress disorder, a very common experience for Vietnam veterans and victims of abuse. She exhibited nearly half of all the symptoms. Nihilism. Drug experimentation. Self-destruction.

Mr. Howard takes off his white carnival barker hat.

BILL HOWARD: We've got a question from a member in the audience.

He skips down the aisle and politely squeezes down the row to a woman and holds the microphone to her mouth.

AUDIENCE MEMBER: I don't have any memories of abuse. In fact, I can't really remember anything. And now I'm thinking, what if this happened to me? You know? Do you think something like this could have happened to me? I'm just wondering.

Mr. Howard walks back up to the panel and holds the microphone in front of Carol's face.

CAROL PORTER: Yes. I'm afraid so.

The woman faints. Mr. Howard worriedly wipes his brow with the hand that holds the microphone and walks back out to the audience. His mustache forms a frown around his petrified mouth as he hunches over a little boy sitting next to his mother. Mr. Howard rests a hand on the child's shoulder.

BILL HOWARD: Our children are at risk. Their lives are in danger. Ladies and gentleman, the children are the future. We must protect our children. *He points his cane at the blown-up photograph of April Laurels.* As many of you know, that girl, April Laurels, killed herself not too long ago to escape the horrors of abuse. She lived a life of unspeakable hell. Raped. Fondled. Forced. Beaten. Shattered. *Mr. Howard pats the boy's head, then looks back up at the blown-up photograph. He walks up to the stage, speaking passionately into the microphone.* I say, no more abuse! *He thrusts his cane forward.* I say, no more violence against our children! *He punches the air with his microphone.* I say, they are the future of the world! *He grunts.* I say, love the children!

The audience goes nuts. Imagine a million screaming girls at a Beatles concert and you're not even close.

[COMMERCIAL]

BILL HOWARD: We have a question from an audience member. Yes, what's your question?

AUDIENCE MEMBER: I just want you to know, Carol, that you have changed my life. My life has always been empty and meaningless, and I never knew why. Everything makes sense now!

Mr. Howard claps along with the audience. He tilts the flat white hat to the side, centers the microphone between his thick black mustache and his lower lip.

BILL HOWARD: Your Honor, I call Meme Lamb to the stand.

As Meme rises from her chair, the auditorium echoes an applause. Meme moves in slow motion, her hips twisting sharply, her feet a full yard ahead of her like a runway model.

AUDIENCE: ME! ME! ME! ME! ME! ME!

Meme sits down at the panel beside Carol, below the photograph of April Laurels. Meme stares up at the multitude of screens with her white face and red lips hovering above the audience. She blinks her foot-long black eyelashes and pouts her Marilyn Monroe red mouth. Mr. Howard silences the crowd by flapping his fat arms. He approaches Meme.

BILL HOWARD: Help me understand the incomprehensible. Through psychotherapy and hypnosis, you were able to dig up memories, to resurface bloodcurdling details, about a past you knew nothing about?

She doesn't hear the question. Meme is distracted, staring up at the screens.

BILL HOWARD: Hello, Meme.

MEME LAMB: Yes.

BILL HOWARD: I know it must be a very difficult thing to talk about.

MEME LAMB: I can do it. I can talk about it.

BILL HOWARD: Are you sure, now? I don't want to force you into anything you don't want to do.

MEME LAMB: I can do it.

Meme moves his microphone downward, so as not to obstruct the camera's view of her face.

BILL HOWARD: Are you Meme right now? Or are you a multiple?

MEME LAMB: Right now I'm Meme, but I think another personality will take over at sometime during the show.

The audience claps.

BILL HOWARD: May I call you Meme for now? *Mr. Howard gently places his hand on her shoulder.* Would that be okay? I don't want to offend another personality in case you switch on me.

MEME LAMB: Yes. I'm sure they won't mind.

BILL HOWARD: Meme, when did you first discover that your childhood was so twisted and sick? When did you first realize you were a victim?

MEME LAMB: When I first met Carol. I already had all the symptoms. I was in an abusive relationship. I suffered from intense depression. There were so many things that were wrong. The symptoms were all there. I just needed Carol to make sense of it all.

Mr. Howard strokes his mustache and pouts for the camera.

BILL HOWARD: Domestic violence! Depression! Incapable of achieving her life-long dreams! *Mr. Howard shakes his head, drops his head, looks shocked before the camera. He bobs his microphone up and down.* Sexual abuse robbed you of the good life, didn't it?

Meme cries into a tissue.

AUDIENCE: Ahhhh.

In the back row is a red and white floral dress wrapped around a three-hundred pound woman with her fingers in her mouth. She whistles.

AUDIENCE MEMBER: I love you, Meme!

More applause.

BILL HOWARD: Meme, what happened to you? Don't be afraid to tell us. Tell the people what happened. Speak freely about the truth.

MEME LAMB: My father raped me from about age one or two, maybe before, I don't have all my memories yet. But he raped me in the cradle, that's my first memory. He ejaculated on me. When I no longer slept in the cradle, he made me sleep in his bed. Though we didn't sleep. That's where he raped me…

BILL HOWARD: We have a question from the audience. *Mr. Howard walks down into the audience.* Yes, what's your question?

AUDIENCE MEMBER: Where was your mother?

Mr. Howard walks back up to the panel. He holds the microphone under Meme's red lips.

MEME LAMB: At first she didn't know. He did it while she was sleeping and my father was quiet about it, real hush-hush when we did it in bed with her. She slept through it all. But when she found out, she wanted to be a part of it. She was upset that I got all the attention. My father wouldn't sleep with her. Only me.

BILL HOWARD: Of course, he also spent time with your sister…

MEME LAMB: He only wanted me. Sometimes, he would make me stay home sick from school so that we could be together…

BILL HOWARD: OK. Let's take a minute to reflect upon what happened to Jill, now confined to a wheelchair and living in the hospital…

MEME LAMB: And he would take me for a ride in the country, to a secluded place, and undress me...

BILL HOWARD: A young flower, plucked prematurely, nearly bludgeoned to death by those she loved and trusted.

Mr. Lamb snorts violently and twists his body up in the chains that are wrapped around his wrists and ankles. He froths and pants, straining his head toward Meme.

JUDGE SEWALL: Order! Order! We shall have order in my courtroom! Stop intimidating the victim! Would somebody please give that animal a tranquilizer!

Judge Sewall slams his mallet.

DEFENSE ATTORNEY: *He turns back toward Mr. Lamb.* Let's be reasonable people. Mr. Lamb, you are accused of raping and sodomizing little girls. What can we possibly say to these charges? Nothing. Because people don't make this kind of stuff up! And even if they did, and this is a more important matter, people do not believe that people make this kind of stuff up. The logic goes like this, they know you are guilty because you won't confess! If you confess...then...uh...this situation is hopeless.

[COMMERCIAL]

JUDGE SEWALL: Court is now in session. Mr. Howard, please continue.

Mr. Howard approaches Meme and rests his hand on her shoulder.

BILL HOWARD: You are a brave woman to come out and speak about this. A very courageous woman! To face your family and say these things, to not be silenced. Let's give Meme a round of applause!

The audience shouts and whistles. Meme waves her hand.

MEME LAMB: Thank you.

Mr. Howard paces the stage from side to side. He moves slowly, as if deep in thought, and then silences the crowd by lifting his hand as a sign to stop. The auditorium falls silent.

BILL HOWARD: Your Honor, I would like to call a couple of guests to the panel. Michelle Agatha, a former client of Carol Porter's, and Joe Morris, an investigator.

Carol leafs through the script in her hands. She becomes restless and fidgety. She whispers to Mr. Howard.

CAROL PORTER: Where's the rest of the script?

Joe Morris and Michelle Agatha enter from stage left and sit at the panel. Joe Morris is wearing a dark suit. Michelle Agatha is wearing a white dress.

BILL HOWARD: Michelle, please state your full name and tell the people how you became involved with Carol Porter and what that experience was like.

MICHELLE AGATHA: My name is Michelle Agatha. I was a client of Carol's. I can't really remember for how long, all the days kind of blur together. I started seeing her because I was having trouble sleeping. I had insomnia. She kicked me out of the group when I lost my insurance coverage. I lost my insurance because I lost my job. I lost my job because her therapy ruined my life.

The audience creates a murmur throughout the auditorium. The jury members look at each other with blank, confused stares.

BILL HOWARD: How did this therapy ruin your life? What did it do to you?

MICHELLE AGATHA: She convinced me that I was a victim of sexual abuse. She convinced me to have nothing to do with my family, to cut off my relations with them. She made me think that I was wanted by a Satanic Cult, which caused me to have anxiety attacks that had to be controlled by medication. The medication made me sick. I couldn't work or sleep, I was so afraid. I lost everything because of her.

CAROL PORTER: That isn't true. She's making all of this up.

Judge Sewall bangs his mallet on his desk.

JUDGE SEWALL: Order in the courtroom! Carol, you'll speak when you are spoken to. *Judge Sewall turns to Mr. Howard.* Mr. Howard, please continue.

BILL HOWARD: Mr. Morris, please state your full name and tell the people what you discovered in your investigations.

JOE MORRIS: My name is Joe Morris. I recently interviewed Carol Porter while investigating the cause of Jill Lamb's injuries. Ms. Porter claimed that the injuries were inflicted by Jill's father, and later exacerbated by child's play. I believed her claims to be inconsistent with much of the evidence, including pictures taken on the day Jill was removed from home. I also questioned her about Jill's therapy session. She denied that it was videotaped. I later received an anonymous package that contained a videotape of that session. I brought it with me, if you would like to take a look at it.

JUDGE SEWALL: Mr. Howard, please approach the bench.

Mr. Howard thumps his way across the stage. He leans closer to the judge and whispers quietly. They both shrug and stare sympathetically at Meme. The judge nods, then pounds his mallet. Mr. Howard wobbles himself around to face the panel. He worriedly strokes his mustache. Stump, wearing a clown suit, walks across the stage floor and hands Mr. Howard a black cassette. Mr. Howard walks slowly along the edge of the jury box, holding the black cassette at eye level.

BILL HOWARD: Judge Sewall has requested that we allow the jury to review a videotape of one of Carol's therapy sessions.

Mr. Howard hands the cassette to Stump. He scuttles to the back of the stage and inserts the cassette in a machine below the back-wall screen. Carol looks back over her shoulder, her face pale and full of despair. Judge Sewall spins his chair, turning his back toward the audience. Jill's purple swollen face spreads across the main stage screen. A face shot so close the scratches on her face look like deep incisions.

"I want to go home."

Meme's eyes roam the auditorium in search of a screen made in her image. A screen with her face on it. Her knees knock and buckle. She falls to the stage floor. A stunt for attention.

"Please let me go home."

Mr. Howard holds a fat paw over his mustache. He shakes his big head. The jury gasps loudly. A few jurors stand up, holding their hands to their mouths. Mr. Howard points a black remote control at the machine in the back of the stage. He fast forwards the tape.

"I love my mom and dad."

Mr. Howard fast-forwards again. An anatomically correct penis appears on the screen.

"Play with it. It won't bite you."

Fast-forward.

"If you don't start talking, Jill, you'll never see your family again. Your mother and father will spend the rest of their lives in prison. And you'll spend your little life camping out in at least a hundred foster homes before you reach the age of sixteen. I'm giving you one more chance to save yourself and your helpless parents. Tell me what I want to hear. Tell me that you were molested! I don't care if it's real!"

CAROL PORTER: I didn't do it! I didn't do it! It's not what it looks like. I was set up! *She points at Bill Howard.* He did it. He made me do it!

Carol charges toward Mr. Howard, swinging her fists at his face. Mr. Howard tries to beat her off with the microphone. Script pages fly through the air. Stars and Blazes blasts through the speakers. Carol is wrested down to the floor by a hoard of security guards.

CAROL PORTER: That's not what really happened! That man is just an actor! He's a fake! They're all fakes!

Her face is pushed into the floor. She continues to mumble. Handcuffs are slapped on her wrists behind her back. The guards drag her away kicking and screaming.

Meme's face is returned to the screens. She flutters her eyelashes and grossly trembles her lips. Her chin is raised and posing for the masses. She licks her cherry red lips and stares out at the concert hall of mirrors reflecting her likeness. Each screen offers a different angle, a unique version, a new way to look at the same thing.

Mr. Howard removes his hat and takes a bow.

BILL HOWARD: Thank you! Thank you! Don't forget to tune in for the next season of "The Greatest Show on Earth." Meme Lamb and other victims of quack therapy will talk about themselves and testify to their experiences. And don't miss "Bill Howard's Reality TV Law & Order." We'll have some fighting Mastiff dogs on trial for eating a child! See ya next time! You were wonderful!

THE END

Epilogue

STOP AND SMELL THE FLOWERS

The secretary says that Mr. Howard is ready to see me. She opens the door and lets me into his office. Mr. Howard is wearing a dark blue pinstriped suit and a yellow tie that hangs loosely over his stomach. His hair is thick and wavy without the grease slicking it back against his scalp. He sits behind a desk made out of a ton of glass.

"Frank," Mr. Howard says, "I'm so happy to see you. How have you been feeling? Please sit down."

I sit down in a red leather chair opposite his desk.

"I read your last letter," Mr. Howard says. "I've read all of your letters, however illegible. However hostile." He leans back in his chair. "You want to experience something more authentic? Something more genuine?"

"Yes," I say.

He rocks back and forth. There is a long stretch of silence.

"What do you have in mind?"

"I would like to experience something that's not commercial," I say. "I would like to feel again. To have feelings that matter."

He chuckles. The flaccid skin around his neck moves downward and rolls like a wave over his collar.

"You are too solemn for words, Frank," he says. "You've written a thousand of these!" He thumps a thick stack of letters, bound tightly with rubberbands, on the top of his desk. "All this stuff about wanting to experience something more real, wanting to live life more passionately. It's what everybody dreams of!" He leans back in his chair. "And that's why I've called for you. I want to talk to you about your self-inflicted isolation."

"The protest," I say.

"Okay," he says, tapping the end of a cigar on the glass desk. "The protest. Of course, Frank."

He looks at me, very gently, at the tattoo stamped across my forearm: HUMAN.

"What you've done to your apartment, it is ingenious," Mr. Howard goes on. "The mirrors especially, the way they alter the camera angles, the way they play with shadow and light. And your late night performance of Frank Sinatra's 'All of Me' is a masterpiece. The way you sit naked in the middle of your room, your body distorted into a cubist sculpture, singing that sad, slow echo of a voice into that flashlight you hold in your hands. I can't describe the feeling of hearing it, Frank, but I suppose it's like taking heroin; the way you make Sinatra's words sound so melancholy is blasphemy. Sinatra without the sentimentalism; it's sacrilege. The first time I heard it—it made me kind of sick. And I have to admit that, for perhaps a day or two, I thought you had finally gotten to me. I thought that I would have to pull the plug on you. But something else happened. The ratings were phenomenal! The people loved it! They waited all day just to see you twisted in your own light like a ghost made of shards of glass, pushing needles into your skin, through different parts of your body!" He pulls out a large roll of paper. "So this has been the fruits of your public bloodletting, Frank. The protest, as you like to call it. You are my greatest success!"

Mr. Howard unrolls a glossy poster across the desk. The title at the top is printed in blood red letters: *The S&M Show*. I'm kneeled down in the center of a room. A light shines beneath my face, illuminating the eyes of a rabid animal. Naked bodies layer the background in an orgy of suffering and gnashing of teeth. It looks like the dark, icy depths of hell.

"We could take this a step further, Frank," Mr. Howard says. "Up the ante! Add a few more people and lock the door! See what happens in there! It could be beautiful!"

Night after night of piercing pins into my body like a voodoo doll. And for what? I've got more scars on my arms than hair follicles, and now I'm a somebody? What has happened to the world? Is it that ordinary suffering has become unrecognizable because we've made a mockery of the saddest things imaginable?

Is there no longer anything significant to report because tragedy is impossible when the media gets involved?

"*The S&M Show?*" I ask.

Mr. Howard smiles and lights his cigar.

"Come on, Frank," he says. "Lighten up a little, will you?"

Mr. Howard pulls me up from the chair and ushers me toward the door with his hand on my shoulder. I step outside his office and walk away without saying anything. Mr. Howard calls out to me.

"And Frank," he says, "try not to take life too seriously. Take some time and think it over."

A tall vase of roses sits on a table outside the office. The stems are made out of green wire; the oversized red buds are plastic. I pull one from the vase and hold it up to my nose as I walk down the hall. I sniff at it for several seconds, waiting for my olfactory organ to experience some kind of sensation. But there is none; it smells like nothing at all. The gesture, I realize, is absolutely futile.

0-595-33427-X